REYES
& LEEDS

BY

FRANCIS VOIGNIER

Cover design by Francis Voignier
Background image: iStock

This book is a work of fiction. Any relation to living individuals, at the exception of public figures, whose names are respectfully used in the context of their professions, businesses, and/or social influence, is purely coincidental.

Library of Congress Cataloging-in-Publication Data
Voignier, Francis 1954—United States
Reyes & Leeds/Francis Voignier
ISBN-13: 978-1-7345551-6-5
ISBN-10: 1734555165

Fiction – Metaphysics – Love – Philosophy – San Francisco – Point Reyes – Marin County

francisvoignier.com
Dolosse & Writs, Eureka, California

LIST OF CONTENTS

INTRODUCTION

The story of Patricia Reyes and John Leeds didn't come to page until the moment I sat at the computer with the odd feeling an inner voice was trying to speak. I am not exactly saying that I channel my work, but in a sense, the writing comes from the deeper layers of my being. I presume a similar process exists for each artist, and one might say that life itself is a channeling affair.

Symbolically speaking, the two characters in the tale may represent the male and female in each of us, genders that seek to express without the interference of an overbearing mind. The core of the story is about trust, and the faith that one's choices are responsible for the paths that lie ahead. The general sense of it revolves around the power of attraction, oft-unspoken greater purposes, and the love that is the driving force behind them.

I hesitate to call the book a love story, even though it is one, mainly because the central theme pertains to a philosophical dialogue between two souls in search of answers through the process of validation, one only permitted by those able to listen without putting themselves in the way. Patricia and John are such skilled listeners, all the while never losing their integrity and sense of humor. In an odd way, together, they represent a whole I very much yearn to become: an honest, giving, and loving self, able to receive without the burden of distrust.

Tuesday, May 15th 2018

I – THE FARE

One never knows when fate puts two people in each other's path. Or does one?

It was a cold rainy day at SFO. The wind was mangling umbrellas and sending bedazzled travelers after tumbling fedoras, flying baseball caps, and crumpled newspaper pages.

John Leeds had arrived from London on Air France. He was in town for the convention at Moscone Center, a one week affair concerning cutting-edge medical equipment. Mainly, he was interested in the advances in robotics for the operating room. His profession: senior researcher at the Department of Clinical Neurosciences at the University of Cambridge.

It was one of those inevitable afternoons when cabs were in short supply, but eventually Leeds found himself tucked in the backseat of a yellow Ford Crown Victoria.

"Where to?" the Latina driver asked.

"The Fairmont, please."

"D'you like talking or should I just shut up?" the thirty-something female asked.

"Anything, but the subject of medicine," the Englishman replied, somewhat amused.

"You're here for the convention?"

"Indeed."

"OK, I already blew it – no medical reference!"

"It's alright, I know much about slipping," the passenger returned, laughing.

"Thanks for being human," she teased.

"I'm John Leeds, by the way—and you are?"

"Patricia Reyes, born in Mexico, reared in the Mission District. You're English, right?"

"How did you guess?"

"The weather you brought with you," she laughed.

"Yes, it seems to be the norm whenever we, Brits, travel. A book should be written about the phenomenon."

"Where in Britain?"

"Outside London—Cambridge."

"So, you teach the unmentionable subject?"

"I do occasionally. Mostly, I lecture when I don't do research. So, now, you know what I do."

"I assume you're married with children, but let me know if I'm being too pushy," Patricia said.

"Not at all, I favor candid over reserved. No, I'm no longer married, while my one grown child is somewhere on a quest to unlock the mysteries of his inner world. But tell me, since I'm of the belief that most cabbies drive to finance their labors of love; what's yours, Patricia?"

"Damn, you didn't ask about my marital status; is that too risqué a question for British prudery? Whatever, I'm between relationships and I'm gay—now, you won't have to wonder. As to your asking, I'm a writer, among other things," she replied, winking at her passenger from the full-width rearview mirror.

"Splendid—what sort of writing?"

"Books."

"About?"

"Life, people, philosophy, politics—I fictionalize what I see, hear, and touch."

"Wonderful—I write as well, but I doubt the contents of my literary excursions would interest you. I'm primarily into what a lot of readers refer to as boring

2

scientific jargon. But unlike you, I don't have to drive taxis to finance my labor of love—it comes with the job."

"What makes you say that driving isn't a labor of love—after all, I meet interesting people all the time?"

"I have never known a cabdriver who didn't have a plan for a way out of the profession, but I could be wrong. Are your books being published?"

"Self-publishing's the way to go—the big houses have turned their backs on talent."

"Isn't it a bit harsh?"

"Sorry, I guess your publisher is one of them."

"Indeed, Pearson—one of the ten big ones across the pond. So, if I visit the Amazon website and type Patricia Reyes, will I find your books?"

"You should, and I suggest you buy all six of them—not to mention that you must write ultra-positive reviews after you read them!"

"And if I don't?"

"You'll be joining the crowd," she laughed.

— o —

Patricia Reyes drove the yellow Ford up a very steep Taylor Street, before turning right on California.

"I guess it's where we part; it was fun having you for company," she said, as she dropped her passenger at the Fairmont's main entrance.

"Perhaps you could join me later at the Top of the Mark, across the street, for cocktails. After all, you said that you wrote 'among other things.' I'm left somewhat curious about these 'other things,'" Leeds offered.

"The Top's a bit above my social status—plus, your curiosity might cost you," she warned playfully.

3

"Don't let the illusion fool you. As to the dangers courting my curiosity, I reserve the right to be the judge."

"I like the sound of that—what time then, doctor?" she teased.

"What about eight, writer-who-drives-taxis-as-a-labor-of-love?" John Leeds countered.

— o —

Patricia Reyes couldn't get John Leeds out of her mind for the rest of her shift—she was anxious to meet at the popular bar overlooking the city and the bay. There was no attraction between her and the fare—there never would be—but something unusual was tugging at her thoughts from across the dark of the back door. It was she, rather, who was curious about the Englishman. He seemed different—nothing like she had imagined a typical British scholar to be. Of course, she realized that she was merely profiling, for she was in no position to know what a typical Cambridge professor was like, having never met one. In fact, she knew little about the English, since those she came across with at parties seemed to have no interest in her kind. If anything, she found them a bit condescending—though nothing to write about. But she had once visited the UK in her youth.

On the other hand, John Leeds forgot about the cabbie the minute he got to his room. He phoned friends in London, reached a few contacts in San Francisco and Silicon Valley. Patricia Reyes reemerged much later, after he had a nap and took a long shower. Refreshed and relaxed, he was glad to have company on his first evening in town. He called room service to order appetizers from the menu—he never drank on an empty

4

stomach, not even a single drink. He ate his food, superficially glancing at the Chronicle's entertainment section. Perhaps Reyes would be interested in going out after a few cocktails. He brushed his teeth and left the room at ten to eight.

— o —

When Patricia Reyes entered the lounge, barely a few minutes past eight, John Leeds was directly facing her. Yet, he failed to recognize her, having overlooked the many ways people could transform based on purpose. The cabdriver had switched the plain, functional mask of her temporary profession, for a much more colorful, special-event one. Interestingly, she considered she came as herself, naked and mask-less, but it was too early for that, since she had brought her shields with her. In fact, those shields were her all-time protectors, especially around men. For the occasion, she had switched the woolen, plaid shirt for a silk one, let her lustrous black ponytail down in undulating cascades over the epaulettes of her faded bomber jacket, and wore slightly loose jeans as to not reveal too much of her perfect ass, jeans tucked inside snakeskin boots that used to belong to her grandfather on her mother's side.

John Leeds was jolted out of his reverie, as his eyes registered the apparition as being his date. He almost stood up to greet her, but she had sat across him before he could unfold his body.

"What're you drinking?" she asked as a greeting.

"Black Bush on ice."

"Ah, Irish whiskey owned by Casa Cuervo; you decided to meet me halfway!"

5

"I guess so, since my mother was born in Northern Ireland—what are the odds? Nice to see you again; I thought for a second that you had no reason to not stand me up," he smiled.

"It crossed my mind, but something told me it would be a mistake."

"That's putting a lot of trust in a stranger."

"Strangers are my turf and you're in my town—I trust I have the upper hand."

Patricia Reyes ordered a virgin Mojito and asked for the small bites menu.

"So, if you don't mind me asking, what is that 'something' that told you it would be a mistake not to meet?" John Leeds asked.

"Ever heard of the intuitive? We, females, have a direct line to it."

"I'm familiar with the term, since my son, James, has been brainwashing me with his views on the whole holistic approach to living."

"And how does it make you feel as a dogmatic man of science?" she probed, playing.

"A good father has to be first an attentive listener and a faithful validator of ideas, as far-fetched as they may be."

"But did they help you change your views, or did you just assume his would eventually realign with yours as being the voice of wisdom?"

"I see what you mean by having the upper hand—yes, they forced me to reevaluate my outlook at what I had deemed to be the irrefutable truth. They challenged me in ways I was poorly prepared for. It was an uphill battle for the longest time, since I wasn't ready to accept that he had a grasp on a reality that had fully escaped me, mostly because I had blindly refused to acknowledge its existence."

"Good for you—and you're still in one piece!"

"So, no alcohol for you?" Leeds sidestepped.

"I don't need it—I'm high enough on life."

"Does it mean you never tried?"

"Be serious, man, of course I tried! As a matter of fact, I tried too much. But at least, it taught me to recognize the line that must never be crossed. I soon realized I was hanging out with the wrong crowd and playing a character that wasn't me," she replied.

"So, you are presently you?"

"To the best of my knowledge, I am the one I wish to stick with."

"Interesting you should put it that way—are you observing yourself from the outside in?"

"I observe myself from within, it that makes any sense to you."

"Right, of course, how could it be otherwise?"

"But then again, John, what do we know of spatial reality? Inside, outside—what's the reference, apart from a subjective notion of a central placement of thinking?"

"Now you're speaking like a cross between a scientist and a philosopher."

"I flunked science, but I'm OK with philosophy."

"But something tells me that you're not totally blind to basic scientific principals..."

"Is that intuition on your part, John, or is it deductive thinking in all of its glory?"

"I also have a line to the intuitive, as poor as the reception may be," he responded, poking.

"How old are you, John?"

"How old do you think I am, Patricia?"

"Umm, you call that an answer?"

"Being rhetorical—I'm fifty-two."

"How old d'you think I am then?" she asked.

"Upper hand again—alright, thirty-three."

"Wrong, I'm thirty-eight; but thanks for picking wisely!" she returned, laughing.

"You want some of this?" she pointed at the assortment of bites the waitress had deposited between the drinks.

"No thanks, I ordered from room service before coming here. I guess I could have offered to meet in a proper restaurant instead," he apologized.

"Not to worry, you said cocktails, didn't you?"

"Correct."

"Is that British to aimlessly apologize?"

"By the sheer number of 'sorrys' you hear in a day in London, I'm inclined to concur. But I would argue about its insincerity—I think it's a sweet way to acknowledge your fellow humans in a crowd situation."

"I wasn't referring to crowds, but same difference. I agree manners are important, as long as they come from an authentic place."

"What do you know of authenticity, Patricia?"

"What about regretting nothing on your deathbed—is that too rhetorical a question?"

"Man, you're mangling me—have mercy!"

"What I said about being the one I wish to stick with—that's what I know of authenticity. Making the choice and knowing it's the right one."

"So, you are showing your true, authentic self to me, am I correct?"

"I'm showing some of it, as opposed to a lie. I can't fully drop my guards, especially with a man, and pretend to be authentic. That's why I don't get drunk, because you and I would end up in your room having sex, and you'd be fucking a me that lied to both of us all night long."

"What about passion, doesn't it play a part?"

"Alcohol doesn't just fuel passions—it unleashes repression in the process."

"And you would know that from experience?"

"Exactly! Authenticity never leads to regrets."

"But what makes your personal authenticity right to the rest of the world?"

"Nothing, it's just a trick question—I can only account to the self."

"Even if it leads to harming others?"

"Then, we're dealing with a false affirmative—something pretending to be authentic, while in the throes of justifying repression through twisted logic. An authentic self cannot hurt the world that supports it; it would pertain to an oxymoron," Patricia said, firmly.

"What if your authentic self made others uncomfortable, hurt their feelings?"

"I can't curtail to guilt—their hurt is theirs, and only theirs to deal with. They'd be creating that discomfort out of their lack of authenticity."

"I asked all of this mostly because I wanted to make sure we were on the same page, or rather, I needed a second take on something I had been trying to convince myself of. So, I appreciate your candor; it's quite helpful at my end—thank you!"

"The pleasure's mine—it's not an easy subject."

"I first came across the nature of authenticity with James—at least from a conscious standpoint. I had always considered myself an honest man, one without hidden agendas, and reared with a strong backbone of ethics by irreproachable parents. My view of authenticity was one of doing the right thing for the collective cause that was 'England first.' Of course, it was the end product of national brainwashing by people benefiting from the taxes of those they brainwashed—like here in the US—like everywhere. I came to the painful realization that authenticity had nothing to do with what others expected of me, or me being an exemplar of good citizenry. To the contrary, it became obvious that I had been living a lie, that my choices weren't really mine, but those that I made, believing they were. True, they were still mine in the end, but I had empowered myself to make the wrong ones, or reversely, disempowered myself from making the right ones," John Leeds confessed.

"That's a mouthful, mister, but yes, I sympathize; you and I are in similar businesses. Based on what you just said, would you consider yourself being your true self in this very present?" Patricia Reyes asked.

"More than ever in your presence, since you seem to inspire me to be just that. It's not always true for other occasions, I confess."

"Like tomorrow when you have to put the doctor's mask back on?"

"It's not the doctor's mask I worry so much about, but the one I have to put on to hide what I don't want others in my field to see. I have come to doubt all the posturing that passes as the health system. After all, we know little about healthy individuals—we specialize in sickness. We don't care to know how healthy people stay healthy, in spite of the obviousness that they seem to shy the medical system altogether—not because they don't need it—but because they have made the concise choice of wanting nothing to do with it. Almost as if that choice were at the foundation of their physical wellness."

"But how do you explain fixing bones and stitching people back together—the injured sure need able hands?"

"I'm addressing a fundamental issue of mass beliefs fueled by the powers in charge of dispensing fears and drugs, not one of medicine at its noble core. I'm afraid my field has come to believe that it exists above the natural order."

"I agree with you, but people decide what's best for them. We have to respect their choices, even if in the end it means a form of disowning of their personal healing tools."

"We still operate as a hive consciousness. It is the responsibility of the pioneers to educate the masses and not exploit them—that is precisely my point," Leeds said.

"So, you're saying that the medical system should still seek to empower its patients, regardless?"

"We are failing at remembering the most fundamental axiom of our field: that we learn from the way the body does its job."

"Many of you think the body is doing a poor job."

"It's only because we are not integrating the various branches of knowledge. The body doesn't manufacture sickness; sickness is oftentimes the symptom of something else, be it trauma, fear, or the surrendering of those healing powers proper to the self. At the far end of the curve, sickness is part of the healing process, not the aggressor. We look in all the wrong places."

"I'm inclined to think you're in the process of betraying your field, John, but then again, you're in the right place to make the appropriate changes. I'm sure there are others in a similar position."

"Yes, there are, but I believe we digressed from the subject of authenticity."

"It sounded right on the money to me."

The option of going out was settled by the rain that relentlessly pounded at the vast expanses of glass. They ordered another round instead, Leeds electing to go alcohol-free as well, with a bottle of Clausthaler to chase the Black Bush.

"I guess you're foregoing getting drunk tonight—anything to do with me?" Patricia probed.

"Yes and no—I don't see the point of riding different waves at the cost of communication. I believe in equal highs."

"You choose wisely—I was trying to figure out my exit route in case you became belligerent."

"That settles it then—a toast to clarity!" John proposed buoyantly.

Patricia Reyes left for the ladies room, affording John Leeds the opportunity to muse on the nature of the rapport between the two of them. What had motivated his desire to further their discussion in the cab remained obscure; yet, it was precisely because of that obscurity that he was able to detect the markers that lay ahead of him and his guest. They, apparently, had business to conduct. Whether that business had anything to do with logic or not was inconsequential. The only other option was to make a perfectly lousy excuse for never meeting again; but running away from something that was pulling at the cloth of his curiosity was no longer integral to his person. If anything, his son James had seen to it. So far, their rapport had been a match—a meeting of the minds without the encumberment of the heart, and he had all the intentions of keeping it that way, even in the face of Ms. Patricia Reyes looking particularly attractive. He couldn't help notice she wore no makeup—a mask he was thankful for its absence. She was gay—that settled it.

Patricia looked at her face in the bathroom mirror—she liked what she saw. It had been a long time since she ran away from herself. The black and blues were gone, the dark rings under her eyes from fatigue and drug abuse, the puffiness of her cheeks and the bloating from alcohol, all gone long ago. Yet, she didn't fear the memory. She had made a clear choice—an authentic one. She felt good, empowered—strong. John Leeds was a fascinating man; she liked his demeanor—neither forced nor lacking firmness. She applauded the fact he had had the courage to reevaluate his stance, taking advantage of an opportunity to change for the better. Not that many dared leave the comfort of their paralysis, the soothing numbness caused by justified fear. She sensed he was ready to make the leap, even at the cost of his status in the field of cutting-edge neuroscience. He could easily end up making a fool of himself, but she trusted his sense of timing was sound. She returned to the table, refreshed.

"Anything new since I left?" she joked.

"This lovely maiden offered her skills, but I explained to her that I had company."

"Too bad you sent her home so quickly—I might have liked her," Patricia teased.

"The thought crossed my mind, but she vanished in front of my very eyes before I could convince her to stay."

"I appreciate the consideration—anything else?"

"Should there have been something else?"

13

"Don't tell me you didn't think about the two of us sitting atop Nob Hill with barely a reason to be seen together."

"How does it qualify as something new?"

"It all depends on what you made of it."

"I thought you were particularly attractive, since you're asking."

"I like a man with good tastes—thank you for having the honesty to say you looked at my ass."

"And yes, I have also assessed that we might have something we share, but I don't have the foggiest idea of what it may be."

"I don't believe in accidents, John, and I embrace the opportunity to discover what it is you trust we share."

"If you're not in a rush to leave, I would be grateful for your company for a while longer. I was asked by some colleagues to join them in the lobby of the St. Francis, but I would much prefer to remain here with you, without the weight of a mask."

"I'm comfortable here and I'm in no rush to return to an empty space, as sacred as it might be."

"Would you mind talking about gay life; my son James is also gay. But you don't have to," John asked hesitantly.

"You don't have to be shy about asking; there's nothing special or sensitive about it. I love women because they're beautiful, and though not all of them are worthy of trust, I feel safer around them than around men. And no, my father wasn't abusive to me; he just wasn't around. At worst, I felt abandoned."

"I'm only interested in you, not homosexuality as a topic. The only thing that needs talking about the subject, centers on societal stigmas. I have no desire to further the narrative—too many viewpoints for my taste. I love my son for what he is, I embrace his gayness fully."

"I guess you needed to let that off your chest. Trust me; nothing offends me in that regard. Authenticity breeds no conflict—try to remember that!"

"We're good then?"

"We're good, John. It's not because I sleep with women that I have never had sex with a man. As a matter of fact, I have had plenty of it with them. It's just that I have a hard time letting go around them. You may find it odd, but there isn't enough female coming through in them—and I know it's there—just that they aren't allowing that side of them out."

"I could interpret it as not allowing the male to come out of you as well. Is there any validity in that?"

"You hit it on the head, John! It's a marriage of opposites; I want to play with the girl in them, but they don't want to touch the boy in me!"

"So, Patricia, it sounds like a male issue?"

"The whole world is a male issue—I hope I don't have to spell it for you."

"I'm aware, and I wish it weren't so. The male hubris is an anomaly that should have left us long ago, but the forces that carry it have gained so much momentum over the eons, that its parabolic curve seems to stretch into infinity. It needs to be broken before the damage is too great."

"Nice to hear it from the mouth of the horse, but your scientific chart scares me. Male dominance ad infinitum is a nightmare incarnate, a tragedy of the highest order, a bane to the human promise. I don't see how we can survive another hundred years of it!"

"We won't—it's a bloody catastrophe!"

"So, how do we break it?"

"It'll take most women to say 'enough!' and more than a few men with the guts to forego all what they hold as true. It's already started, with sexual abuse making the news. With luck, it'll tumble your present president—he's the grotesque exemplification of the stigma, a total disgrace that must be brought down."

"I agree. But those are just words, and judging by how nothing is actually being done in spite of all the noise, I don't see much breaking on the horizon."

"You have a better idea?" John Leeds asked.

"I have this crazy theory that though we can't change this particular course, we could always choose another one..."

"I may have an idea of where you're trying to go with this, but I can't push forward until I'm sure of it— too slippery if I'm wrong. But if I'm correct, we're about to enter a rabbit hole. So yes, take me there!"

"It's just a theory, John, now you're being dramatic!" Patricia laughed.

"Take me there anyway."

"OK, it's unprovable if it works—same if it doesn't, because you would never know whether it did or not. You're either in one place or the other, or yet, another. With faith and determination, we could already be there. Are we there, John?"

"I love a good riddle, Patricia. Alright, because I wouldn't know whether I'm there or not, I have to go on the faith that I'm already there—therefore, I am."

"Not bad, John, do you want to be there, on a course steadily snaking away from the madness of man?"

"Definitely, Patricia—are we there?"

"Stop making fun, it's for you to answer!"

"OK, I believe we are."

"Look at me in the eyes—are you sure?"

"We are."

Patricia Reyes took a sip of her second virgin Mojito, while John Leeds leaned back in his seat, bearing the look of a man that had just come out of hypnosis.

"How curious, can you explain?"

"That was you being your authentic self. Don't go back where you came from, John, there is nothing there."

"What do you mean?"

"I'm only telling you that your choices are sound; that's all. Keep on following that inner voice."

"For a second, I felt pulled into a mental vortex; I must be getting tired," John said.

"You're the one who mentioned rabbit holes and asked to be taken there, don't you remember?"

"I do, but I didn't expect an actual experience. I thought you were just going to tell me about your crazy theory. But yes, I asked for it."

"Telling you would have just been words, like the ones you write in your books. A good theory is one with teeth—it can't be explained in sentences."

"So, you induced a sort of trance, correct?"

"I don't have those powers, nobody does, but you do, in regard to yourself."

"I think I'm getting it. It just took me by surprise."

"Good, for a second I thought I had misread you; that would have been kind of odd."

"It was a long second."

"Time's relative, John; there are even places where it doesn't exist—maybe you went there?"

"If I did, I surely would know. It's been a very long day, I'm sorry, but I must regroup."

"Metaphorically-speaking, one that stretched all the way to England—quite understandable. But don't be sorry; I'm ready to leave. Here's my card if you wish to connect again—no pressure if you don't; I won't take it personally," she said, getting up.

"Fair enough—thank you for the company," John Leeds returned, finally feeling the mounting exhaustion, while knowing he had much to prepare for before actually going to bed.

Patricia Reyes walked away. She didn't look back.

2 - THE SECOND DAY

John Leeds woke up at seven with the feeling something undefined was missing. Room service came in with the morning paper and a hearty breakfast meant to put order in his thoughts. He was confident the omnipresence of vacuity would soon refill with the more pressing details of his reasons to be in town. He had left Reyes' card by his iPhone on the dresser, weighing the options of reconnecting versus not. Their time together had been fun up to the point of his short quasi-lapse in consciousness—a detail he strained to comprehend. Technically, she had nothing to do with it, but his guards were up nonetheless, as if she had touched something that was meant to be left undisturbed.

He wasn't due at Moscone center until ten, when he would attend a lecture on the advances of 3D printing materials and techniques in bone reconstruction, a subject he found far from stimulating, but he had questions that needed answers. His next lecture was at two—the last one, at four. In between, he would check booths and meet with colleagues from around the world.

He entered Patricia Reyes' number in his iPhone's contacts list, giving it no particular thought—something he had done so often that it had become an item of reflexivity. He had met numerous strangers across his many travels—one-night-stands that never went further than brief, temporary memories—short blips on a chaotic background of events in the processes of construction and deconstruction—relationships that clawed at time, while others pulled away in spite of their tethers. For the moment, the cabdriver was one such blip. But John Leeds also knew in the back of his mind, that resistance was at work—he was in no small part running away from her. She had come too close in too short a time. His natural transformation was gradual, gentle—she, on the other hand, represented the fracturing of his being, something he had no power over, or rather, his mind had no power over. He wanted to do it his way, on his schedule, but a small voice from the depths was already reminding him that at the rate things were going, such transformation might never happen. He swiftly slid the thought sideways to return to the convention's schedule.

—— o ——

Patricia Reyes had picked up her cab from the lot at five a.m. She had only slept four hours, but she felt alert and joyful. The rain had relented to make room for a magnificent sunrise over the Oakland hills and the bay. There was no better way to wake up and be born again. She had sensed the Englishman had pulled away towards the later part of their meeting. She knew why—it happened to all of them. Hell, it had happened to her many times. To reinvent the self was a process that required more than the flighty desire to reap the benefits without doing the actual work. It took courage, and the strength to stand up after each failure. But failures were never truly failures—they were markers, or even better: steps forward that had all the appearances of going backwards. When negativity, or denial, or more generally, fear had been in charge for so long, everything appeared to run in the wrong direction—positive stuff et al. John had had a setback as soon as the *shift* happened. He had

20

mistaken victory for defeat—his mind had. She was aware he knew what had happened, but he hadn't expected it to be so close to his reality—something he had accepted in theory, more than he had actually conceived it being an item of everyday occurrences, something that usually happened in the absence of knowledge. A thing naturally taken in, that the mind would reject if it knew it were there. Likely, the mind—the intellect—was just pretending it wasn't there. That thing—or *shift*—happened with each fundamental adjustment to the mental process in regard to one's private reality, with each belief updated or replaced by another. They weren't just mental shifts; they were experience-altering phenomena that ran a lot like the point blades of a railroad track switch, but a lot smoother. She passed the Mark Hopkins on her way to the Embarcadero, acknowledging one such shift had happened from mutual choice the night before, hoping doubt wouldn't send the both of them back to where they started. But she was confident she was there to stay, with or without John Leeds. Her Android buzzed over the traffic noise.

"Just dropping a fare, I'll call you back!"

She hung up; not even checking who had rang.

She pulled up to the curb by a café in North Beach, got out, and bought a refill for her thermos. She leaned back in the cab, checking her cell phone screen. The displayed international number left no doubt John Leeds had called.

"So you didn't run after all!" she greeted.

"I'm left with a half answer; I insist on collecting the other half—what about later sometime?"

"Sometime's OK, what about somewhere?"

"It's a deal; see you there!" he joked.

"I'm glad you didn't lose your sense of humor over my incursion into your private world. I'm sorry if I pushed the envelop somewhat, but then again, you asked for it, if memory serves."

"Not to worry, I'll survive. It's just that we might have to go back into the rabbit hole—it appears I left something in there," John said.

"From where I stand, that thing needs you more than you need it, but it's up to you—you have the whole day to think about it. What about we meet at La Taqueria on 24th and Mission, at seven; you're down for comfort Mexican food?"

"Sounds splendid, I'll be there! I must now put the mask back on—see you then!" he exclaimed cheerfully.

— o —

John Leeds, instead of running away, as Patricia Reyes had implied a few hours prior, had come to terms with the reasons of his discomfort. Namely, he had taken charge of the situation, something that generally occurred after a setback. He was one to keep his spurts of depression short and harmless. Now, he was ready to see to the depths of what had happened the night before—that curious experience that was felt as if time had been reset without affecting its placement or momentum—as in—someone came in and replaced all the clocks. He admitted to himself that what he had left in the "rabbit hole," was none other than a yearning to return to safety, a fear of change that Patricia had aptly unveiled in the words of "it needs you more than you need it," a fear that cried for sustenance, for a support platform rich in rationalization, for a stroking of confidence that ironically and shamelessly sapped at confidence itself. She was right; there was nowhere to go where they came from. But had they really switched courses, or was it yet another of those skillfully crafted illusions the mind was so illustriously renowned for? The thought rang of doubt—it had to go. Reversely, he convinced himself that what he was looking for existed in the nebulous zone between him and Patricia Reyes—each in possession of one half of the code that unlocked its hideaway.

— o —

They found an empty table in the back of the busy Taqueria on which they set their fares. John Leeds had forgone the suit for black jeans, a tan embroidered gunfighter shirt, and a tweed jacket. Patricia Reyes wore an open, soft plaid cabin shirt over a tank top that left little to the imagination, while she casually carried her bomber jacket on one shoulder.

"You forgot your cowboy hat," she said.

"When among the natives, dress like a native," he replied.

"You should have thought of it when it mattered; it could have changed the course of history."

"Sorry, it was meant to be funny."

"I get it, John."

"You disapprove of the outfit?"

"Not at all, you look good in it."

"Am I allowed to say you look stunning?"

"Were you forbidden?" she teased.

"British etiquette, you know."

"I assume we're not here to stroke each other's egos; I'm at peace with my looks and I don't think you need to worry about yours. I hope your day was productive though. How did those bone-making machines pan out?"

"Surprisingly well—sound technology with lots of potential in the field of neurosurgery; especially in assisting with the reconstruction of shattered skulls, if you should know."

"Sorry I asked; it sounds gruesome. But I observe it did you good. So, John, can you tell me what changed since this morning?"

"What makes you think things changed?"

"You sounded like you had just made up your mind about meeting again. Now, you feel like you've settled comfortably into that choice—a small nuance, but a nuance nonetheless."

"True, Patricia, last night I believe you came too close to my chamber of secrets, and too stealthily for that matter. But then, today, I had to admit to myself that I actually walked into the situation."

"Honesty is a strong ally—I appreciate your aptitude and willingness to see beyond the proverbial knee-jerking. I'm used to people freaking out around me. The thing is that I just can't tolerate the general bullshit that passes for conversation these days. Why hide when there's nothing to hide? We're just fucking human! Problem: we've stacked the deck so high with useless beliefs that we don't even know what's there—we accept all kinds of shit without ever thinking. Like you said yesterday, we're looking in all the wrong places. I'm not even sure we know what we're after. Tell me how many times someone has asked you a question and walked away—you can't, right? The game is so engrained that we forgot we wrote the play. Anyway, you don't seem to be one of them, and I'm thankful for the little time the cosmos is granting us, so that we can share what we know," Patricia said.

"By knowledge, I don't assume you mean the scholarly stuff... Yes, I too see ample posturing and projection, and very little honesty about the self. Lies abound while the truth becomes the subject of derision—I'm not exactly sure I understand where the taint comes from. Most likely, it falls into the category of historical, stigmatic male dominance we briefly touched upon last night, but I don't believe it's worse than it's ever been. To the contrary, I see it as a case of increased consciousness on the part of those willing—and more are. Allegorically speaking, we're overwhelmed by the crap we've created. But until we stop blaming our perceived enemies for it, I'm afraid we're not going to progress too rapidly with the cleanup," John Leeds imparted.

"On the topic of male dominance, what's your take on a version of the world under strong matriarchal rule, say—d'you think it would be just as bad?"

"You kind of answered the question—but yes, I believe it would, since it appears we strive for balance. On the other hand, it's inevitable things must swing the other way first—it's a necessary evil. I wish I could say women alone can save the world, but it's not a belief I wish to nurture. Though as a first step, their collective strength will be needed to straighten the ship. You and I will be long gone before the race finds its equilibrium."

"But you understand why some of us would want you guys to live on one side of the planet and leave us alone, don't you, John?"

"You have all the reasons to feel that way, so yes, but I don't thing it's the answer. I trust your strength is in realizing that you have more power than you ever allowed yourself to think you had. You fell to the male ego like a population to the idiotic rational of a dictatorship. Too many or you became acceptant and even complicit—you had the strength all along, but the betrayal towards the female spirit is apparent throughout history. Alright, I'm not saying the male ego can get off scot-free; to the contrary, it must too harness the female energy back into its core. Of course, it's an overly simplistic view—so much harm has been done that I can't even fathom where to begin," John said.

"What's done is done, we're not gonna rewrite history, but we can script a new one with better actors. I look at our government and I want to puke. How is it even possible that we should have these clowns ruling the country as they wish—all of them pathological criminals! And look at our press secretary, you call that a woman?!"

"That's what I mean by complicity; these women are doing a lot of damage, but then again, they're not the main culprit—the old mad cock is still ruling the roost. There's an intrinsic fear at the base of it."

"You say it's not worse, yet in spite of the fight, it's still there in all of its sickening glory."

"You have a point. Five hundred years ago, you would have stood no chance to enter in an open conversation with a man on male dominance, and now you can. Yet, could it be that women's emancipation is still part of the same narrative—just a veneer in the line of, 'They're more easily controlled when they think they're in charge'?"

"You have a way with stirring mind fucks, mister, but yes, there is some of that—a when-you-can't-fight-them-join-them kind of deal. It's obviously another maze that could see us disappear into and never return. What d'you say we move away from the subject for a while, so that we can regroup with better ammo?" Patricia proposed.

"Yes, it's tied to a multifaceted issue whose side I'm not sure to tackle first, so saving it for later sounds about right. What if we talked about you instead?"

"Only if you promise to return to where we left off last night."

"I was afraid you'd say that," he humored.

"You're not walking away, John."

"I can take it."

"So what d'you want to know?"

"Yesterday I said I would ask you about the other things you do beyond writing—here we are."

"My life is a canvas, John. I'm trying to figure out how I ended up painting it that way. That's at the base of all the things I do. I actually paint. Some of my work hangs on the walls of a few coffee houses around the city. I could take you there, or I could bring you to my studio to show you; but then, that would require more trust, and I'm not sure we have enough time for that. I paint about life—small works within the larger one, if you know what I mean. I think of them as fractals of a complex whole, private windows into an incommensurable oneness of being. Some are joyful, some not. They're moods, waves; one minute static, the next, as fluid as the winds that race through the downtown corridors. To you, they probably will just be colors on a board; but to me, they churn great emotions, passions, moments of sadness, and others of elation. I wish they could become as alive to those who see them as they are to me, but then again, I doubt they would summon the same forces to their hearts. In essence, they would become their images. That's what is said about an artist letting go of their work—it is not theirs, only their hands are, or their voice. We're the messengers of the spiritual, the ones with the farthest reach into the source of being. At best, we are the observers of our art in the making, at worst, its victims. The choice depends on the emotional and psychological strength of the artist. Some see the creative flow as an intrusion on the self—it ties into what we spoke of a moment ago, the same stuff that everyone is exposed to. Life can be play or work, but not in the usual sense... It revolves, once more, around authenticity. I'm an observer that marvels at the process—my mind is—because it's at peace with not being in charge, and trustful that it's integral to what is..."

"Please continue, Patricia, you have me in your spell," John said, taking a bite out of his taco.

"Since you put it that way, I'm also part of a drum group—all girls. That's another level of fun and creative altogether. Timbales, a cowbell, and a cymbal, just like Sheila E; that's my rig. We're thirteen in the band. Needless to say, we make a lot of noise. The point is, we mesh into a single beat, a one voice, a soul greater than the sum of our individual ones put together. Once again, it's a form of return to the source, to bring back joy and harmony into the world. You know what I mean, John?"

"I do, and I'm awed by your creative drive and outlook at life. So, let me ask, Patricia, is the larger painting beginning to make sense?"

"It does a bit more every day, with every beat, every stroke, and every time I have a chance to share with someone like you: a willing ear married to a word of validation. It's not always easy living outside the box—not just style-wise—but philosophically as well. I'm aware everyone is, in one form or another, doing their best to make sense of reality. But there's a fundamental difference between those who look at the world as something outside their view, and the ones who hold that world within them. As part of the latter group, I feel accountable for staying focused, aware that my every moves are sending ripples in all directions, and that, eventually, these ripples will reach far shores and leave patterns in the sand. That world is never taken for granted, for it is integral to my health and sanity. If I mistreat it, soil it, throw my trash around, roll coal my way through existence, I'm the one who will have to deal with the cleanup. In my view, it's the best way to remain socially responsible, but it has its drawbacks, especially in the light of the first group not being as careful about their environment and, ultimately, themselves... Am I making any sense at all?"

"You are and I could listen to you all night long, but you have hardly touched your food. I suggest we take a break from the hard topics, since I'm the one who got you started," John humored.

"Ha, you're right, John, I could go on and on about that stuff."

The eatery had become so busy that a line ran all the way to the back, where they were sitting. The noise level had also risen up a few notches.

"It's getting a bit loud for conversation, John, we should probably go somewhere where we can hear each other; plus, I think they could use the table."

"Do you want me to call a cab, we could take a ride to where we can see the sunset, for once there's no fog—what about the Cliff House?" John proposed.

"We might miss the sunset, but I love the idea!"

It only took minutes for the Yellow Cab driver to call their names. On Patricia's recommendation, they went up a steep Clipper Street to Portola, and then down Woodside to Laguna Honda and 7th Street, into the Sunset District, and finally, through Golden Gate Park, to the Pacific. The sun was setting on the horizon by the time they made it to the Dutch windmill, across from the beach. They decided to hike down the trail to historical Sutro Baths from above the Cliff House. Upon reaching the bottom, they sat on a rock overlooking the ruins.

"It won't be long before it gets dark, but we'll have the benefit of a full moon soon enough, if you don't mind sticking around for a while," Patricia informed the Englishman.

"Don't you have to get up early for your shift?"

"I only have a set two-day schedule. Depending on how much money I make during that time, I decide on whether or not I need to drive the other days. For now, I'm good; so I'm technically off tomorrow and, possibly, the rest of the week."

"So, if I get it right, today being Wednesday, you don't have to work until Tuesday?"

"Correct, so I will paint, write, and drum my heart out," Patricia replied with a laugh.

"A sane way to live, my friend!"

"About last night, John, tell me how you came to get weirded out by the bit about changing course?"

"Oddly, I felt entranced by your words—akin to some psychological switch being engaged. I can't quite define it, but it was as if time had played a trick on my mind and I found myself in a new place, not remembering how I got there. But obviously, I was in the same spot I had left only seconds prior. So, it made no sense," John Leeds replied, looking towards the dimming horizon.

"And it makes sense today?" Patricia probed.

"Not that it does, but I have settled into the notion that it was just one of those things that happen occasionally, and which we forget with predictable regularity. Like waking up from a dream and having a difficult time returning to reality."

"Which reality would that be, John?"

"You're asking as if there were more than one."

"There are, so which one do you think is the one you treat as your primary one?"

"I would imagine, this one, if I actually believed in multiple, overlapping realities."

"But you do, don't you?"

"I confess that I have seriously contemplated the possibility, but science is having a hard time getting a handle on it. Though, I believe quantum physics is having a field day with it."

"I sense not all of science agrees with science, if that's even a concept."

"Well, it's mostly scientists having issues with other scientists. They don't always concur. Actually, some of them don't like to see their beliefs challenged— just like the rest of the population. It's another element of human conditioning and behavior via a fear-based set of silent and blindly accepted principals. Irrespectively, science will keep on pushing and usher the scientist away from rigid axioms and closer to the more amenable world of philosophy, which, irrefutably, he or she will try to turn into a fixed science. We always return to the same point, regardless of where we start, don't we?"

"Well, you might be generalizing a tad, John. There are plenty of brilliant thinkers among your people. I believe you are making a picture of your own combative self in regard to change."

"Possibly, but to my credit, I said 'some scientists'; hence, I trust I am far from generalizing and putting my good name and conscience on the line. Plus, I am confident I'm not the combatant you speak of."

"Yet, you still wear the mask among your people, which indicates part of you is at odds with your desire to adapt to change."

"I see; you're not going to leave me alone with this, so yes, I am admitting to some resistance. Are we allowed to move on, now?" he asked, amused.

"As I said, I'm a hard interlocutor, but I can still apologize. So, sorry if I stepped out of line."

"All good, Patricia."

"Since you have contemplated the possibility of multiple, simultaneous realities; where have you arrived at with it, and how is it weighing on your existence at large—philosophically speaking, that is?" she asked.

"In some barely lit corner of science, what you are referring to is the field of probabilities, emergent options from a single point in time, based on individual and/or collective choices; and not necessarily strictly human-generated, since the biological and larger cosmic makeup aren't exempt from choice-making. But at our level, it translates as a seamless system of ever-changing lanes, meaning that those realities are not simply multiple, but nearly infinite, which, of course, makes of life something far more complicated than what we have ever allowed ourselves to imagine. A surgical choice, one that is married to purpose and aided by a focused mind, should theoretically be able to create such a switch. But it might take practice long before it becomes a conscious process. So, in that line, I believe it is what happened last night, because we both wanted the moment to change, unencumbered by doubt, right there and then... Does it answer your question?"

"Part of it—you're forgetting the bit about how it is affecting your personal life."

"Well, as you mentioned last night, those changes are mostly imperceptible. When they happen, nothing seems to have occurred, though to the more aware among us, these *shifts* don't always go unnoticed, because they tie into the constantly reevaluated framework of beliefs. The more willing you are to look at the self, the more adept you become at consciously actualizing change. At my end, it's mostly a theoretical reality, since I have been, so far, unable to perceive such changes, at least, until last night. How it has weighed on my life is now a matter of how able I will become at tying that specific experience to my past, and pinpointing other similar instances. For now, the present will suffice, since it seems to encompass all others."

"Up to this point, simultaneous presents were not part of the narrative, now they are. You're a resource beyond my wildest expectations, John."

"It's only because, I am finding the space to express—everyone's too busy with their lives, Patricia."

"I make the time, John; that's why we exist together in this moment. It just happened you were looking for that space. I don't think it's just wishful thinking on my part to believe us meeting is no accident."

"I want to agree, but had I landed in a different cab at the airport, it would have been no accident either. If the man before me hadn't lost his hat to the wind, you and I wouldn't be here tonight. What I am saying is that there are no accidents anywhere, anytime—only various plays on the theme of life, variables contingent on myriad elements, all connected from infinite, minute angles."

"But we still experience the moment as a singularity. So yes, and irrespective of all the other plays, this moment between us is still no accident. It reflects where we're at, privately and together, at this precise intersection. Your scientific mind might want to make a complex map of it, but my heart seeks to streamline it to its basics: the here and now."

"In other words, you distill it to a single beat on your drums?"

"That would be a potent analogy if it could hold, but a one beat is a 'happening,' the effect tied to the cause—it being my choice to hit the drum within that particular slice of time. A true analogy would be at the level of the drummer, and not that of the wave generated by the warping of the skin from impact. If I had hit a bell instead, perhaps the performance would have been altered. So the analogy would have centered on the result rather, and not the hit. Let's not forget the greater impact of purpose—the man could have lost his hat because of both our desires to meet, even though we had never been made aware of each other. It doesn't only mean that we already knew of each other's existence, but that we are connected by purpose, the one of enriching our lives with new knowledge and affirmation, but also of sending ripples into a world whose aspirations are to draw on that knowledge itself, be it another book I write, or you doing advanced work in your field. But what does it make of the man with the hat—an accomplice, a willing actor? Or was the wind the accomplice? And who made the wind, John? You were the one there, experiencing the moment from your own standpoint; and me, from inside my cab, on my way to you, standing amid twisted umbrellas reminiscent of a chaotic dance of large, wilted Morning Glories. Now, focus on just the two of us, isolate the picture from the rest, blow it up, and tell me where the actors are and where the writers stand... Do you get my drift, John?"

"I get that you are taking me down another rabbit hole, but luckily, I am familiar with that one," he laughed.

"So, then you know exactly what happened last night—you're aware we're no longer on the course we were on when we started the evening, right?"

"I can't deny we're onto something. Somehow I'm able to see things differently with you around. It seems to be a lot easier for me to doubt the self without some form of exterior validation. With my son James, I became used to leaning on him when my rational mind got in the way. In a sense, I relied on his belief system to make adjustments to my own. You might call it a form of symbiosis. I think that's what's happening here, Patricia."

"It doesn't matter how you shake it, you're still in charge of making your own choices—the methodology is nothing more than a personal approach to it. What counts is the desire, the drive to cross the imaginary caution line and get to where the real work begins."

"Let me ask you then, are you always this clear about your convictions—just curious?"

"Good question—if you want an honest answer, it's no, I'm not. It's not easy to admit, but no..."

"Thank you for your candor, it helps to know."

"Now that you have exposed a vulnerability, could we observe a moment of silence to take in what's around us, in this sacred now?" Patricia requested.

There was barely a glow on the horizon. John Leeds sensed something similar to what had happened to him the night before was now weighing on Patricia

Reyes, a retracting of the self, a retreat of the forces that only a moment ago had stood victorious. He could have wrapped his arm around her, since they sat so close to each other, but he knew it would have been a mistake, an assumptive maneuver over the sanctity of an inner meeting. Instead, he listened to the crash of the waves.

— o —

Patricia Reyes broke the silence with a laugh. She stood up, taking in the gentle breeze that blew from the waters. It was a perfect spring night in the Outer Richmond district—no fog or wind, no penetrating cold from the frigid ocean. She was ready for a long walk along the beach, perhaps all the way to Sloat Boulevard and the zoo. It was a lengthy stretch, over three miles—well worth it for its mind-cleansing effect.

"You want to walk, John?"

"That'll be nice—where to?"

"Along Ocean Beach—all the way to the zoo!"

"I once stayed at Robert's, on Sloat—one of the funkiest motels in town. I believe it was torn down a few years ago and replaced by a large concrete building."

"You seem to know a lot about this town for a foreigner."

"I come to San Francisco at least once a year. I've been doing it for the last two decades. I also studied at UCSF for three semesters—excellent neurosurgery department with top specialists."

"But why Robert's, the place was a prostitutes and drug dealers' hangout?"

"I like the real world, what can I say? You don't know about a city until you've met its shady characters.

Hardship carries substance, at least, that's how I see it," John Leeds affirmed.

"Same with me and the cab driving."

"So how long do you thing it's going to take us to reach Sloat Boulevard?"

"Probably a couple of hours—you're up for it?"

"Why not, it's not like I need much sleep to walk the aisles of the convention center with my notepad."

"What about your colleagues, don't they wonder why you're not spending any or your free time with them?"

"They know me well. They'll say that John is on another one of his adventures; I'm certain."

"So then it's true that you're not like them."

"I'm a researcher by trade as well as nature. I seek to probe the vast unknowns, which sensibly explains why we're in each other's company," he jested.

"Do you seek to probe my depths, John?" Patricia asked, amused.

"I'll refrain from letting my mind analyze the roots of the question, my friend, but platonically-speaking, and with your permission—yes."

"Wise answer, John, but between adults, I trust we can humor the self."

"Then, you are saying that we have managed to build a modicum of trust between us."

"I feel comfortable around you, so I guess I trust you, which doesn't happen often for me around men."

"I'm honored then."

"You should be, John, you should be..."

They walked down Point Lobos Avenue to the first beach access. The sand stretched all the way to Daly City, past Lake Merced. The moon had risen to the east, over the faraway and no longer visible Oakland Hills.

They took their shoes off when they reached the edge of the brine.

"Here we go—woo-hoo!" Patricia exulted, running in whirls on the wet sand.

John felt a similar mounting élan within him, but refrained from demonstrating it—though he made a mental note that perhaps he needed to unstiffen.

"Does the beach always do that to you?" he asked.

"Not always, but when we, girls, get together, it inevitably becomes a dance party. You guys need a football or a Frisbee to help you loosen up, don't you?"

"Yes, it sounds pathetic!"

"I guess, being from Cambridge, you don't have much access to any beaches. Do you ever drive to one?"

"Ha, we've got the River Cam along Midsummer Common, but no sea. The Channel and the North Sea are miles away, but when time permitted, James and I drove down to Brighton, about twice the distance to London. It sounds like a long ride, but in American distances, it's just a stone's throw away, a hundred and twenty miles, if memory serves, but too many bloody tolls. On a good day, it's only a two hour drive. One may say that England's a small place, made large by people with big imaginations," he humored.

"I visited Britain once with one of my girlfriends, a rock singer in the vein of Crissie Hynde, who wanted to move there and make a name for herself. I think she became shell-shocked by what she saw. It's funny how the mystique loses its veneer the minute reality kicks in. I don't know what ended up toppling her castle—maybe the surplus of male chauvinism. She was too glad to return to the relative safety of San Francisco. As to me, I left her in London and traveled north, all the way to

Inverness. I enjoyed Scotland quite a lot!"

"Normally, that's the first question people ask each other: have you ever been there or done that? It only crossed my mind when we were already deep down the rabbit hole," John uttered.

"If you say *rabbit hole* one more time, I'm gonna scream. No more rabbit holes, please; I'm done with clichés."

"How is it a cliché, it's a pretty clever term for what it is intended to describe. Doesn't it originate from Alice in Wonderland?"

"Maybe it's too clever; I just don't want to fixate on the term—why not 'down the mole hole'?"

"As you wish, but it seems it hit a raw nerve."

"I have many raw nerves. As I've mentioned, I have a low tolerance for the reflexive stuff, the things we say without thinking, or because we think it's cool to say them. I'm done with the insincere use of language. Sorry, I just don't like the term anymore. Or maybe, I no longer enjoy making fun of something as serious as doing our homework in regard to returning to the source of our reason of being. There's been too much escapism, too much humor thrown in for the sake of avoiding facing the music. I just don't want that between us," she explained.

"I get the point, Patricia, but please, don't get bent out of shape because of it. Allow me to have my sense of humor, if you want me to validate yours. You just had a mood swing, if I may say so."

"Sorry, John, I own my shit," she apologized.

"We're good, but you took me by surprise."

"Let me be frank with you, I'm not used to being that close to a man emotionally—I think it scares me deep inside, even though I said I trusted you."

"I understand, Patricia—think nothing of it. Let's just take a deep breath—we don't have to say anything for a while," John offered.

"I'm sorry, it was just bratty on my part, I don't know what took me," she confessed.

"So, what did you like about Scotland?"

"I don't know; it had a different vibe from south of it—more ancient, but also clearer, as if the past were still breathing through it—hard to explain."

"I understand what you mean; the place is rich in barely stirred history. It's a place were the stones still speak. Ireland used to be the same, but not as much anymore—too many people have moved there, displacing spirits; as least that's what is being said."

"Don't you believe in spirits, John?"

"Not in the sense they are aware of our presence. I believe in bleed-throughs, if you know what I mean."

"I guess you're saying there are not aware they can be perceived by us."

"Something of the sort, but I still have to find someone who's dead-certain they have actually seen one."

"I believe it's mostly because most people are projecting. The spiritual reality is somewhat more sophisticated than the BS you'll find on the front page of the Enquirer."

"I'm aware of that. My take is that your common spirit is more like a temporal print, a residual element of something once solid, or more precisely, an aspect personality left behind by the confused ego."

"That's a first, John; I've got to remember that one!" Patricia voiced exuberantly.

"That's what happens when nobody interrupts to talk about the weather—it keeps on coming,"

"That's the soul talking, man, just like during drumming, writing, or painting. You're simply channeling—get used to it. As one would say, you don't need to kiss that stone to acquire the gift of gab—you were born with it."

"Don't tell me you visited Blarney Castle!"

"Just a bus ride from Cork, my dear friend."

"You are full of surprises, Patricia; what brought you there, certainly not the quest for eloquence?"

"Ha, no, I was on my way down from Scotland, coming through the Lake District into Wales, and at Swansea, I decided to cross St. George's Channel to Ireland. I landed in Wexford and took a train to Limerick. From there, I got a ride to Tralee, and another to Dingle, where I stayed at a bed and breakfast for a week. Then, I managed to hitch another ride to Cork. After a week in the city, I called Air Canada to have my return flight switched from London to Paris, and then I boarded a boat to Roscoff in Brittany. Finally, if I remember correctly, I caught the fast train from a town called Morlaix, to Rennes and the French capital," Patricia enumerated.

"Wow, that was an education; you went through it as if it had just happened yesterday. When were you there?" he asked.

"Oh my, that was in the early aughts. But it's true that I have an excellent memory."

"Impressive—I bicycled around the Dingle peninsula, so I'm a bit familiar with the area. As to Brittany, I stayed with friends in a lovely town called Binic, not far from Morlaix and Roscoff, as a matter of fact. What are the odds we even crossed paths?"

"Yes, in the cross-blur of two extremely fast trains," she teased.

"Math-wise, it sums up to a three hundred and sixty miles per hour encounter, but easily negotiable with freeze frame. Hold on, it's coming back to me—I remember your face, Patricia Reyes!" he laughed.

"So, now you're having fun, science man!?"

"Boys will be boys, dear."

"Wanna take a dip in the surf?" she proposed.

"Isn't the water a bit cold for that?"

"Not enough for a quick dive—it's one of our rituals with the girls."

Patricia Reyes stripped naked—she looked lovely in the moonlight. John Leeds followed her; unsure of the legality of swimming on a public beach in the nude, but then again, there wasn't a soul in sight. The water was utterly freezing, even for an Englishman, but he was brave enough to immerse himself completely before running back to the warmth of his clothes. Patricia stood, facing the moon for a while before she dressed—just long enough for John to feel a mounting sexual desire and the beginning of an erection—a detail that didn't go unnoticed.

"If I may be so blunt, when was the last time you had sex, John?" she enquired, after they got dressed.

"Is that even a question, Patricia?"

"I witnessed your arousal, that's why I ask."

"Are you seeking to embarrass me, or are you that comfortable with the topic of male genitalia? I could just say it was a mere reaction from the jolt of the water, but I would be lying. Frankly, I found you extremely desirable when you just stood there. But I'm behaved enough to keep my passions under check. Though, if you should know, the call of pheromones is still an honorable one. As to your question—too long ago."

"Don't be alarmed, John, I'm the one who

instigated it—I'm simply honored you find me attractive. But I must confess I was surprised by my own impulse to stand in front of you and give you ample time to scrutinize me in my most intimate. I can't say that the attraction is not mutual, which doesn't mean we should fuck here and now. I think there is an exquisite quality to existing in a state of controlled sexual tension. I hope you don't think I'm completely full of shit," she said, somewhat apologetically.

"I can't say it's your standard situation, so maybe, we should run it off—fancy a race?"

Patricia and John ran the remaining of the distance to Sloat Boulevard. They arrived exhausted, collapsing on the sand with relief and laughter. They both realized they had come close to seeing through something they had promised themselves to not fall for—maybe later when the deeper purpose reached completion. Patricia called a cab. Before long, they ascended Portola and dropped down Clipper into the Mission, where Patricia resided at 21st and South Van Ness. They hugged. Fifteen minutes later, John Leeds was dropped off at the lobby of the Fairmont, drained but feeling complete.

3 – THE THIRD DAY

Patricia Reyes got up in the middle of the night—she couldn't sleep. She had masturbated in the shower, aroused from some place rarely visited. Her body felt like the skin of her drum, flexing under the hit, in slow motion, warping in the shape of the first wave about to be released into space. She thought about the beach; how she had desired the Englishman, counter to what her mind had advised against. For once, she was willing to challenge the choices she had made regarding relationships with men, her fear of them, her distrust in them... John Leeds had slammed open the door, unintentionally, unaware. He had relit the candle that brought light to the space between the male and female of her soul. She liked what she saw, but she also felt it wouldn't last; that by morning, whether it'd be from fear or a new assertion of male untrustworthiness, she would be driven to scale down what they had achieved on that stretch of moon-soaked sand the evening before—that rationalization would step in to right a wrong. Yet, morning neared and, deep down, the churning was still hard at work—fear and joy were sharing a dance.

— o —

Though he felt refreshed from uninterrupted sleep, John Leeds awoke amidst the semi-chaos of his incomplete thoughts. He likened it to a hangover from intellectual and emotional overload. Patricia Reyes, in spite of the lovely time they had together, had confused him. The push/pull of her complex personality had stretched him to his limits. He found the candor and rawness of her questions overbearing; yet, he also realized that there was nothing in them that was fundamentally unsound—just that her kind of honesty was, at times, too brutal—too savage.

One of them would call, or perhaps neither would. It all leaned on the precarious balance of what was to come next: the convention, his involvement with the trade, his colleagues. He found the thought comforting. For once, since he had arrived in town, he recognized the value of the professional choices he had made—he didn't yen to run away from them as he had become accustomed to in the last couple of years—especially since his bitter divorce. These choices were calling him back, back into the fold of the relative safety of the familiar, back to a place where there were no Patricia Reyeses, no wild forays into the abstraction of probable outcomes, no sexual innuendos followed by mind fucks—he was free of the illusion of freedom, of the alluring seduction of the unordinary. Paradoxically, wheedling voices were drawing him away from the zones of the predictable, the logical, the sacred commonality of a system of mass acceptance... His reasoning was confusing him. He was two John Leedses, "No, make that three, or four," he thought. The twisted winds of annihilation were whispering the radical suggestion of blocking Patricia's number, of terminating the rapport, of aborting the mission. "Aborting the mission? What a strange concept..." he realized. But "mission" was indeed the key word to the fast rewind of the last few minutes, back to that obscure pool of neglected or abandoned contrivances, the place where the latest gang of doubts had sprung from. "What mission?" he pondered. He poured coffee and took a bite out of his croissant, resolute to put order to his thinking before he came to a final decision about Patricia Reyes.

— o —

Meanwhile, Patricia Reyes had rung a couple of her friends to arrange for a breakfast meeting at a local, hip eatery. She was met twice with messages. She felt frustrated. So much energy had come to the surface, which she needed to disperse through sharing, and perhaps ritualize with laughter around its release. How foolish she had been to provoke a sexual reaction out of her companion. She realized how unwise and unsafe it had been, but she couldn't convince herself of it. She was attracted to the danger, intoxicated by it. She didn't recognize herself through the emotion. Perhaps, a younger Patricia was calling from a forgotten place, from a lonely beach on a deserted island. How did she end up there, why hadn't she been remembered? But she knew. She knew that in spite of her fear of men, she had cloistered the side of her that was attracted to them, "nunified" a biological need under the necessity of survival. "What a mess," she thought. But could she afford to resume with her relationship with the Englishman? Was it saner to continue than delete? The energy wasn't letting go—she couldn't tell whether the danger was real or just a caution flag raised by the frantic urge of some beliefs to self-protect. At the root of her predicament, the overwhelming vote was for a continuation of the experiment—for that was what it was: an experiment. The term reassured her. It reminded her

46

that the choice wasn't final. Even if it was a mistake, it wouldn't be a terminal one. The alienation would only be temporary—nothing she couldn't handle. On the other hand, if the hidden potential tucked inside their stimulating quid pro quo could benefit the both of them by contributing to the expansion of personal knowledge and awareness, then the risk was well worth taking. She picked up the phone.

— o —

John Leeds didn't have to guess, he was certain Patricia was the caller. It could have been anyone out of the long list of contacts in his phone, notwithstanding the possibility of a solicitor, but the call had already been made on the intuitive line.

"Morning—I knew it was you," he greeted.

"Hi! Then you must already know why I'm wishing to connect this soon," she tested.

"You're freaking out, right?"

"Easy, cowboy, I didn't mean for you to tell me that you had that kind of information," she humored.

"A shot in the dark, but I admit it was a rather tight space."

"You have time for breakfast, somewhere?"

"Technically, I should be heading for Moscone Center to attend a lecture by a colleague from Japan. But something tells me that I already know what it's about and that he's not going to notice I didn't show up—so, yes, why not!"

"Then, if it's OK with you, meet me at Sutter and Steiner, in an hour—you're cool with that?"

"I'll see you there, but be prepared to cancel your

plans for the day, since I am annulling my engagements—do we have a deal?"

"Fair enough, John," she surrendered.

— o —

They were lucky to get a table at Sweet Maple without having to be subjected to the long wait. The popular eatery was crowded, but Patricia had called and made reservations.

"Some of my customers have recommended this place very highly, going as far as claiming it's the best breakfast joint in the city. I trust their judgement," Patricia said.

"It's lovely; but I'm famished—I only had coffee since I got up."

"Same here—I can no longer think straight."

After they made up their minds on what to order, John looked Patricia in the eye.

"Let me be candid—I almost decided to never see you again. I understand we don't have to be sexual with each other, but I strongly recommend we stop pretending it's not there—the feelings, I mean."

"You seem to forget that, last night, I admitted to the attraction being mutual—so, what is there that should further be acknowledged? We both agree that it would be foolish to cross the line—it sounds like a well-defined set of guidelines to me—so what's the deal, John?"

"It's just that it took me by surprise, both you taunting me, and me feeling aroused. I don't want to spoil whatever it is that clicks between us."

"I will only ask this once—how do you perceive us having sex spoiling what clicks between us?"

"A lack of preparedness, conflicting emotions, a lamentable surrendering to our most basal instincts? I don't know; take your pick."

"And if there weren't any of that—would you consider?"

"I can only answer by asking you if you would."

"I would want to get it over with, in order to move on with what we're supposed to accomplish together."

"At my end, I would want to make it integral to the accomplishment. That can't happen with confusion or desperation in the mix."

"Then we need another *shift*," Patricia said, pensive.

"A trip down the mole hole?" he couldn't help querying.

"Touché, John, simply brilliant, but yes," she replied, rolling her eyes.

"Sorry, I was just testing."

"I know, I kind of asked for it."

The food arrived, bringing the topic to a momentary halt. The recommendation was well founded, the fares were as excellent as they were beautiful to look at. John called them a display of live culinary art, which made Patricia smile with reserved affection for the man across the table.

"I need to hammer this once and for all, and then move on with the festivities," Patricia stated. "I want you to understand that I never seek the company of men, or even accept invitations from the best of them. The fact we are here together is nothing short of a miracle—it practically makes no sense at my end. In other words, it was not supposed to happen—but it did. It did, and instead of freaking out about finding myself with you, I'm freaking out about fucking it all up and seeing you gone. It's an inversion, John, and I'm not used to this kind of personal drama. So, please, bear with me if you can. I'm tough, but I'm also fragile. All I'm asking of you is to recognize that I have acknowledged the sacredness of our encounter and that I want to follow through with it, wherever it takes us. So, if it's not where you're at, tell me right now—nothing gained, nothing lost, no-one hurt—you dig?" she finished.

John looked at her intensely.

"Let me take you to the country, then we can probe the depths of what it is that is burning between us. I have called a rental company—we have a car reserved. All we need to do is get there and drive away. The Marin Headlands come to mind, and maybe Inverness and Point Reyes in your honor," he proposed.

"I'm at your mercy, but a ride to Marin sounds sublime. Where's the pickup?"

"350 Beach Street—I reckon we can hop on the Golden Gate Bridge from there."

"Two nights ago, I assumed I was gonna have to play tour guide, but you have it all figured out. Take me around, mister!"

They finished their breakfast, paid, and tipped. The Yellow Cab appeared within seconds of the call.

"Ever use Uber or Lyft, John?"

"On occasion, when someone else makes the call. I understand Silicon Valley has moved to San Francisco and brought their app-based drives with them, but I'm old school and cabs are integral to its streets. Yellow, Luxor, and Veteran's are what I'm used to."

"Well, we had to learn some of those Silicon Valley tricks too, but I agree, real cabs carry a mystique."

"Here we are!" John exclaimed, "Today, I'll be your driver!"

I took less than ten minutes before they reached the mid-span of the Golden Gate Bridge—the red of the vast structure against the headlands offered a breathtaking image of surreal juxtaposition.

"There are great bridges in London, as well as other parts of the UK, but the genius of Charles Alton Ellis existed in a category of its own," John remarked.

"So, you know Joseph Strauss didn't design it— that's impressive! I admire the fact you don't take to bullshit too easily. Imagine the hubris of a man who thought nothing of robbing another of his intellectual property."

"It happens every day; you're a musician—if your creations are out there, you've been robbed," John said.

"So you know about Spotify and the likes?"

"James keeps me informed—he's a keyboardist and composer. He loathes the men behind the heist."

"Good for him!"

They picked up the Shoreline Highway at the bottom of the Waldo Grade, but instead of aiming for Muir Beach, they took a right on Panoramic Highway and headed for Stinson Beach.

"If you see a place you like, you're welcome to ask me to stop." John offered.

"I could use a bush when you have a chance—the coffee's doing its thing."

They both relieved themselves by the roadside.

Back in the Chevy Bolt, John reengaged the original thread interrupted at Sweet Maple. He too wanted it to be over with the elements of discomfort.

"You're OK talking about where we left off,

Patricia?" he asked gently.

"Absolutely, but not at the cost of the scenery, if it's alright," she bargained.

"We can certainly make the two work as a team."

"I enjoy the sound of it. But yes, as I said, it's a first for me to find myself with a man, especially me not being in charge. Last it happened was a long time ago, when I was a different me, or rather, a me buried under the weight of a façade. I found you attractive the minute I met you, all the time thinking it was your charisma that carried the charge. But when we stripped naked on the beach last night, something happened—I was aroused to the point of heavy lubrication, if I may be so descriptive. I felt like a teenager unable to control her hormones. In some respect, your swelling member awoke me to the fact. I'm sorry about the mind fuck, John," Patricia explained.

"I am flattered by your trust, but I am sure you understand this is not the wisest of narratives around most men. Your candor could easily pass for a green light to a non-negotiable sexual situation."

"I'm aware of it, and blessed you're not one of those men. To be able to express at this level with you, is not only highly liberating, but also extremely engaging on new levels; but I'm probably high on some form of hormonal charge."

"You are still in control, I trust."

"I am, but how far can I go with this, before you, John, find yourself no longer in control?"

"No-one ever asked me such a question, and I'm fairly certain no-one ever will beyond today."

"Can you answer it though?" she insisted.

"I am in unfamiliar waters, so I can't ascertain my

nerves are made of steel. But overall, I would say you're fairly safe—so go ahead."

"If I didn't feel, deep inside, that I already knew you, I wouldn't speak of it. As a matter of fact, I would have ran away the second I dropped you at the Fairmont from the airport."

"Ditto, kiddo—I considered the option a couple of times already."

"Since we agree that we can't escape each other and that we feel a common attraction, how are we going to be able to not fuck each other's brains out?"

"Perhaps we can't, or maybe, after we finish talking about it, the whole thing will have lost its luster."

"That would be the easy way out," she humored, somehow reassured by the casualness of John's response.

"So, about that *second shift*, Patricia, has it happened yet?"

"It's in the process of happening, John."

"How can you be so assured?"

"We wouldn't be here otherwise."

"And that determines it?"

"Would you have considered the possibility a couple of days ago; I most certainly wouldn't have?"

"I think you're right about that," John concurred.

"I'm glad you agree."

"But you're correct—how long can two grownups speak about their sexual attraction to each other, before moving on with the deed?" John asked.

"A pertinent question, since what's left to talk about? We sound like two brainiacs nearing meltdown."

"What do you say we trust there's a time and place for everything and leave it at that? After all, it doesn't appear anyone's against it, or for it."

"It only proves the uselessness of the brain when it comes to sexual matters," Patricia asserted.

— o —

They settled into the ride, the scenery, the thrill of knowing the Pacific was churning its dangerous surf a hundred feet below at the base of the cliff that followed the road like a temptress into a mysterious dark. Then, they found themselves at sea level, passing beach houses and spectral eucalyptus trees shaking their long leaves and bark strips to the breeze. They finally arrived at Drake's Beach, on the Point Reyes peninsula—there were only three cars in the lot. They hiked down to the tawny sand and walked half a mile along the sinuous edge of the water, at which point the chance of meeting anyone had become very remote—the world was practically theirs.

"I guess this is the time and place for the ultimate test of will," Patricia said, unsure.

"A test of the nerves," John jested.

As it turned out, sex wasn't the biggest assignment on the list; it was merely a stop along the road. Patricia took off her clothes first, and then aided John in removing his, freeing his erect member from the unbearable tightness of his jeans. They kissed passionately, touching, rubbing against each other, until finally, Patricia begged John to get inside her. Before long, they were both running towards the surf to wash away the fluids of their released passions, laughing— freed from the shackles of imaginary constraints.

"That wasn't too painful," Patricia said as she lay on the warm sand.

"Wise of us to not heed the naysayers!"

"Agreed, perhaps we should do this more often—like now," she invited.

"Well, if you insist..."

They made love three times that afternoon, affirming the potency of their connection. But neither made the false claim of loving the other—they were too sagacious to allow their minds to mangle a perfectly good thing. The phase of labeling the relationship was over with; fear and distrust were forgotten amid the prints left in the sand, and the subject of sex had walked out of the general conversation to be replaced by the items that had formed a line at the door, namely, elements of synchronicity awaiting their due acknowledgement.

— o —

The Bolt barely made it to San Rafael, where it sat at a charging station. Patricia and John took advantage of the setback to walk to Phil Lesh's Terrapin Crossroads for an early dinner of farm to table fares. A local blues band was setting up for an early show, letting out the occasional soft cry of a wah pedal, or the rattle of snare springs during subtle checks. The food was healthy and delicious—both promised to stick to certified organic cuisine for the rest of John's stay, which was relatively easy in the Bay Area. The Englishman invited Patricia to his room at the Fairmont, but she insisted he came to her place instead, convincing him that funky furniture was healthier on the brain than the sterility of institutionalized accommodations. He pressed on grabbing a change of clothes from his room on the pretext their love-making had dangerously compromised his underwear.

"I'm sure there's something at my place that can act as a substitute," Patricia offered.

"Umm, I'll pass on the thong, dear," he replied.

"I don't do thongs!" she cried.

"Cold-blooded British humor—nothing to it," he returned.

"Finally, they made it to her apartment on South Van Ness. It was a lovely place full of plants and colors, mostly from the many paintings that hung from all walls and leaned everywhere against anything that was willing to offer support. John deemed her to be an exceptional painter—he immediately loved her work, complimenting her on her unique talent, and offering a view on the direct effect of its output on his soul. She was delighted.

"I wanted you to come here for two things, first, to see my art, and second, to impress on the notion that *the second shift* is likely complete."

"Let me guess—my presence here would have been improbable two days ago, and that said *shift* required a major adjustment to your belief system for it to come to actualization, am I correct?"

"You're a fast learner, John. To most people, the nuance would be imperceptible—change is change—and they don't question the direction of the winds they believe originate from somewhere outside their selves. They don't understand, or are not willing to understand, the direct correlation between their beliefs and the choices they make, and how that directly ties into various outcomes. When I've tried to speak about it to some of my friends, the reception has varied from lukewarm to downright antagonistic. The denial of the powers of the self is overwhelmingly winning over subtle healing and reason. People are refusing to be accountable for the blatant choices they make, yet they cry when things don't work their way. They lament over a paradox they create from the ground up. But I respect their style; it's none of my business to tell the world which direction it should rotate. On the other hand, if they come to me whining, what am I supposed to do, John—lie?"

"The human ego is inherently simple in all of its complexities—it is unquestionably insecure. It knows of its mortality; that's why it feels challenged by the infinite source of its existence. It is fitted with the gift of creation within the context of the finite, the time-dependent, linear reality we call life. All-knowing of its short assignment, it endeavors to mimic the larger creator, while denying its true presence. Allegorically speaking, the actor rebels against the playwright, insisting on remaining ignorant of the fact he is also the creator of the living script," John voiced, rolling his eyes.

"Tell that to the masses, mister! Women have tried for eons, only to die on pyres, or be demonized for their intuitive. Of course, I'm speaking for the symbolic feminine, and not the friends I mentioned a minute ago. Women are not that much different from men at the ego end of things these days, but I wage they still have a direct link to the source."

"I know what you're trying to say, but it's a moot point, since they're not doing anything about it as a whole. Though I'm aware the courageous ones are extremely powerful women. Speaking of powerful, didn't Starhawk live around the corner from here?"

"She still does when she's not in her other place in Sonoma—we've crossed paths numerous times."

"Earlier, we spoke about the female and the male present within each opposite gender—of the need to reconcile the powerful elements that compose the self. We silently agreed we have a shared responsibility to change the world—or, as we said—create *shifts* that will harness the items of experience and usher them in the direction of a more favorable outcome—all of it based on the premise that adjustments must be made at the levels of individual and collective systems of belief. The two of us have come to a point at which we *believe* we've consciously created two such *shifts* in the little time we have known each other. I am now convinced of it, even though I started as a hardened theorist, which is also short for *curious unbeliever*. All this to say, that whatever *the shifts*, and wherever *they* take us, the previous scenarios still remain active—that the change of outcome doesn't delete the original one. In other words, we are not replacing one choice with another, but rather, bringing something new to the pot, or to the larger experience— meaning we are multidimensional beings."

"You're talking as if you'd been there and back, John. Can you elucidate where this comes from—just curious?" Patricia inquired.

"I said earlier that I too have a line that taps into the intuitive. It's not just the theorist that speaks, but the theorist that is allowing his inner voice to speak. Put simply, my views on the theoretical field of probabilities have created a channel for the truths about its greater reality to come through."

"How certain are you that you're not projecting all of this via the mental process?" she probed.

"I can't afford to doubt the validity of what comes to me through the back door. I have to trust that the inner voice I am referring to is not the one of delusion and deceit—I cannot conceive of such evil. In some way, it would rob us of the fundamentals of our relationship. Simply said, we wouldn't exist in this now."

"As I said, I was just curious. I have trusted that voice for the longest time; but on a few occasions, I ended up doubting the soundness of its message. Every time, the reasons for such doubts came out of unchecked assumptions, or ancient, forgotten beliefs, the kinds that litter the floors of the abandoned corridors of ill-fated experiences—those that require years of therapy to revisit. The added advantage of empowering the self is that you get to become your own therapist. Trust is the greatest healer, and self-love, the most potent of medicines—the reverse works well too," Patricia worded, smiling.

"At the risk of repeating myself, I want to make sure we agree that the reason for being able to express at this level is because of our willingness to listen to the other and validate what is being said. It could come in handy later on for argument's sake, when I venture into sharing my views with my confreres. So, we agree on that, right?"

"We do, John, and I've also said it—we wouldn't be here together without your willingness to hear me. Walls don't talk back—at best, they send weak echoes. That's what it means to exist within a social framework of fixed views, some of them immutable untruths. But a kind ear is one that befriends many voices, affording them to come out from under the cover of their shyness," she replied, putting her head on John's shoulder.

"Thank you, it makes a world of difference."

"You being here, our thought-sharing, our love-making... it all makes a world of difference to me. It's me who thanks you, dear man."

"I know we haven't spoken about this, but I gather I am meant to spend the night here with you?"

"Yes, if it doesn't mess with your schedule too much. But I'm sure you can always swing by your hotel if you need your mask," Patricia humored.

"What is the schedule you speak of?" he jested, "I can practically fake my way through this convention! But in all seriousness though, you're right; I have to get organized around tomorrow—I must indeed stop by my room in the morning to gather my things."

Patricia lit candles and closed the curtains. The rich colors of her paintings assumed depths that called for their exploration. John felt pulled in their direction, into the inner world of Patricia Reyes—into the mysterious recesses of this new, shared reality.

4 – THE FOURTH DAY

John Leeds awoke at 6:00 a.m. to the buzz of his iPhone. Patricia stirred by his side.

"Already?" she mumbled, before pulling the sheet over her and going back to sleep.

He kissed her on the forehead, grabbed his clothes left crumpled on the floor, and aimed for the bathroom. Ten minutes later, he was outside, on South Van Ness, calling a cab amid the tumult of garbage trucks and street sweepers. He was going through the motions, barely focused from a long night of love-making and talking. All he could think about was how he was going to survive returning to the routine of his life in Cambridge, when he felt that the real life was in San Francisco with this extraordinary woman. There was no way he would ask her to come with him to England. She belonged to the Bay Area—her roots, her happiness and sanity were integral to her life here. Furthermore, he couldn't impose his presence on her—the strength of their relationship existed on the fragile fulcrum point of that very short window in time. They obviously complemented each other, but they were presently free from the pressures of being emotionally or financially codependent. He would have to marry her, or someone else, to afford to move to the city; and finding a job, in spite of his impressive curriculum vitae, was at best a timid prospect. He could arrange to visit more regularly, but that would fall on the premise of surrendering to the inevitability of a shared life without the usual intimacy and proximity. The whole thing was unrealistic. They had seven days, give or take a few more that could easily be tacked on, but that was it. They were locked in as long-distance friends, vulnerable to the arrival of others in their lives that would eventually take away the last of the happy memories about once-shared passions and exceptional sex. It was the cost of short encounters—they left the soul with a need for more, a vacuous sense of relinquishing something vital. He rearranged his thoughts to concentrate on the day and the tasks ahead of him.

— o —

Patricia got up an hour after John left. Thoughts similar to his joined in a muted battle across the fields of uncertainty. She could never leave San Francisco, yet, letting John return to England to become a long-distance lover made little sense. The emotion that emerged was one of great discomfort, as if by gaining a friend, she had already lost one. She had entertained the outcome the instant she recognized her feelings for him—hence why she deemed it wiser to keep the sex out of the picture. Thus, she was left befuddled by what she had done by instigating what later unraveled into the Drake's Beach affair. She knew of the dangers then, for it was clear their union wasn't merely casual. The term *soulmates* was best at describing their situation, but she refused to go there. Realistically, John had no valid reasons to relocate to the States, and even if he wanted to, there were too many hurdles—from logistical to emotional—that stood in the way. Also, she would never accept anyone in her life, man or woman, dependent on her for survival for any length of time other than the short transitional period afforded to those with solid plans—though, with that in mind, it wasn't totally inconceivable that a position at one of the local universities should present itself on basis of his impressive professional record. But it was a lot to ask out of a three-day relationship, which also demonstrated how strong their bond was. Ironically, it could also have been the marker for an absurdly potent and dangerous infatuation. She resigned herself to leave it at, "We shall see!"

— o —

John called at noon.

"I can't free myself for lunch, but if you're into it, we can meet after my last conference—it ends at five," he proposed, semi-expecting a *won't do*.

"Say, I join you at your hotel at five thirty so that you can slip into something comfortable before we come up with a plan. I'll read a magazine while you take a shower," Patricia joked.

"Brilliant! I need to run—see you then!"

John wondered if he hadn't been too abrupt. He could have said something nice, like, "It was great spending the night at your place." But he immediately relaxed into the trust of the moment—there was no room for over-thinking.

When he arrived at the hotel, Patricia was waiting for him in the lobby. Instead of her jeans, she wore a floral dress over leggings and a leather belt that hang loosely over the perfect shape of her slightly rounded belly. The whole was topped by the age-worn bomber jacket she never seemed to part with.

They kissed and got into the elevator that took them to the upper floors. John's room overlooked Huntington Park and the squat structure of the Pacific

Union Club. Directly across it, stood a majestic Grace Cathedral.

"I can't say the view is not to die for," Patricia remarked.

"It's even better from the rooms overlooking the bay, but one shouldn't complain."

"With a few exceptions, San Francisco looks great from any angle. I love this city," she affirmed as if to make a point, (or was it John just reading into it?).

"When I studied at UCSF, I contemplated the possibility of residing here permanently, but finances dictated—I couldn't afford it at the time, and my parents already owned a house in the country and an apartment in London, where I could stay for practically free."

"Would you come to live here if you had the opportunity?" she asked.

"It's a loaded question, Patricia—so many parameters are in play. It would be a lot simpler if it were just the two of us without any of the hurdles associated with rash commitments—I would move in with you in a heartbeat. But with enough preparation, the scenario isn't utterly inconceivable."

"It looks like we have another three days or so to get on with what we need to get out of our systems, right?"

"It appears so, but we also have another three days or so to figure it out. Both of us seem to be afflicted with the same angsts, so, hopefully, we'll be working out a solution to this dilemma together."

"You're right, there's no valid reason to succumb to panic," she humored.

"Right on—now to the shower!"

Patricia didn't pick up a magazine. Instead, she

stood in front of the window to look at the expanse of housing that stretched from Nob Hill, through Pacific Heights, and into the Richmond, all the way to Lincoln Park and the ocean, where merely two nights ago, the two of them had their first encounter with irreversible attraction. Indeed, San Francisco was beautiful, and she believed it had stolen yet another heart.

— o —

They went out to Greens at Fort Mason, in the Marina District, sticking to their promise to eat organic for the rest of John's stay.

"It used to take months before you could get a table, how did you arrange reservations for tonight with just a phone call, John?" Patricia asked, somewhat impressed, as they were being seated.

"It helps having friends in high places; plus, remember, we went through two successful *shifts*—all good now," he jested.

"Speaking of shifts, John, I would love to resume with the topic. There are questions in need of answers, if you don't mind me probing your fine intellect."

"These days, my intellect has been sending requests to the department of intuitions. It decided to take a vacation somewhere south of here—Mexico, I believe."

"Or Drake's Beach, at Point Reyes?"

"Even better!"

"That means it's still fairly accessible."

"It's a matter of perspective—I've been having a hard time accessing it personally," he returned, laughing.

"You know what, John; your twisted sense of humor is a big part of why I like you."

"England was built on twisted humor; you should give the place a try one day."

"I already have, but most of their twists are wound the wrong way—yours are just as I like them. Maybe you learned from your mother's side."

"Ha, that's good, Patricia!"

"Thanks, I thought so."

"Back to the *shifts*—what do you want to know that you don't already have?"

"How is it possible to switch outcomes without affecting the past?"

"Simple—it's not. You tweak the present—everything gets touched."

"Profound, but our pasts didn't change when we went through *them*."

"Is that what you think or are you testing me? I thought you said that if the past were to change, no-one would notice because it would be integral to the *shift*. You must already know the answer."

"But I don't know yours," she pretended to beg.

"OK then—the department of intuitions confirms that time is nothing more than a series of presents, forming a smooth linearity, as in the one sequential reality we recognize as life. Now, imagine facing a distinct choice: the first thing that comes to mind is a Y in the road—you either go left or right, both directions sharing the same past. The second option is that you find yourself at an X—at the exact crosspoint—you can either go straight and continue with your existing past or make a turn, taking on the past that comes with that line. That's the ultra-simplistic and basic picture of a matrix composed of many choices and events coalescing into a simultaneous whole. Since all these realities are, in essence, various predictable outcomes imagined by the larger self—the playwright—and interpreted by its actors—keeping in mind the actors are also playwrights of their own—each variation is branded with a single, unique signature; thus, the self recognizes them all as belonging to her/him. What said department of intuitions is telling is that with every change, a new past is introduced—memories et al—that the self identifies as its own. It also says that only in the case of extreme changes—such as in the course of trauma or radical decision-making—do these memories veer substantially from each other. Mostly, we deal with subtle alterations. In any case, the self is rarely aware such tweaking has been made to its past... It's the best my intellect can muster at the time," John said.

"Not bad for a mind that claims to be on vacation. But your department of intuitions is still full of brainiacs. Mine just says, 'Of course the past changes—what's there to explain!?' But yes, John, I suspect as much. I was just thinking about it today—about my fear of men, where it came from—and why, all of a sudden, I'm with you, barely comprehending my angsts, as if they had been totally unfounded. So, I imagined a scenario. Before the *shifts*, say, I had a series of bad relationships rife with abuse. I was raped and beaten—and then I got pregnant. I visualized I wanted to keep the child, but then, 'my man' got enraged and hit me in the guts with a baseball bat, inducing a miscarriage and nearly killing me. He was jailed, and I moved on with a new life, away from men and brutal abuse. After the *shifts*, none of that happened—just an absent father, explaining my distrust in men, but nothing more. So, John, how does it look on paper?" she asked.

"Your department of intuition is so much more organic—mine is akin to a muffler shop," he humored.

"You mean as in the silencer attached to the pipe that juts out of the motor, underneath the bonnet of the mechanical contraption that comes with *tyres* and a spare in the boot—is that what you mean by muffler, John?"

"By Jove, Patricia; it didn't take you long in the UK to harvest our terminology for the anticipated purpose of making fun of us, did it?"

"As I said—I twist the other way."

"Would that be the Mexican twirl?"

Patricia almost choked on her lettuce, burying her face in her napkin to tame a burst of laughter.

"Are you alright? I didn't mean to kill you with a pun," he said, both concerned and amused.

"The perfect crime, John—death by laughter."

"Better that the ice bullet by far!"

"Please stop, or I'm going to wet my undies!"

"Waiter, we have a situation—too many diuretics in the food!" John playacted.

"Stop!!!"

"Sorry, I couldn't help with the last one—doctor's humor," he apologized, touching her hand.

"Once more, I asked for it—got to look into the pattern. I can't instigate and ask for mercy at the same time, can I?" she half-joked.

"It all depends on magnitude and context. But in a world full of evils, your plight stands as a lesser one."

"You think the world is full of evils, John?"

"Not at all, it's just a way of saying—I don't even believe in evil per se."

"Good, me neither—at least not fundamentally, like the devil, or whatever superstitious nonsense."

"So to regroup, we agree that past is integral to outcome—both future and past get 'rewritten' from the standpoint of the present, correct?"

"Until further notice, meaning, when someone comes up with an argument rendering the idea obsolete."

"You're aware, of course, that many thinkers and non-thinkers alike will find ample reason to beat that notion into the ground," he hinted.

"They can beat all they want; it's their ego they'll be pounding. I only answer to reason, even if I disagree with it—manners first!"

"So, you're good with being proven wrong?"

"Anything that helps me move forward—knowledge is never static for very long. A minor setback is a chance to garner momentum and propel the self onto the next level."

"Pure wisdom, Patricia—you are indeed a philosopher! Is it the sort of subject you explore in your writing?"

"As I said, I turn all that shows up in my environment into fiction. Fiction meaning, the intuitive exploration of all the hidden folds of the psyche."

"So, in essence, what you are saying is that your environment is a projection of your inner world?"

"Ah, you're getting warm, John! Exactly, that's how you come to understand the power of beliefs!"

"By accepting the world as a projection?"

"Correct! I know it's a hard sell, but I'm irreversibly sticking to it"

"So, according to you, it means that we have it all backwards?" he posed, intrigued.

"Look around, John, look at the results of conventional thinking—does it look right to you?"

"Dare I say it's a bit radical to claim the eye doesn't see and the ear doesn't hear, but rather, project what the mind mistakes for perception?"

"That would be the argument of human logic, but it's also the same logic that accepts war, inequality, sexism, racial divide, absurd religious rhetorics, political bullshit, et cetera, as business as usual."

"But science has a handle on the reality of perception, the field is extremely sophisticated and absent of the kind of logic you are referring to."

"Human logic is human logic, educated or not. As long as it accepts the bullshit around it, it will keep on lying to itself. The belief system dictates the rules around perception and projection, and I'm telling you, those rules are rife with logical fallacies. The eye projects what the mind wants to see. You're welcome to think about it," she challenged.

"But how can you explain what I'm hearing you telling me...?"

"All the more power to my point," she stamped, claiming a win to John's dazed delight.

— o —

It was on their long walk from Greens to Crissie Fields, along the Marina, that John approached the subject of the inevitability of a *third shift*.

"I'm not comfortable with the idea of returning to England and not seeing you for another year. I don't think phone calls are ever going to make up for the lack of physicality. If you feel the same as I do, now is the time to think about tackling our dilemma. Since it was deemed improbable for the two of us to meet, not to mention the love-making, a course of events, dare I say, only realizable via the specifics of bending some of the old beliefs, we need to think about what it will take to turn seven days into forever."

"Yes, John, I agree. It's a good time to take a close look at what we have and be honest with each other. We've only met four days ago, so the idea of commitment at this conjuncture is still considered insane by most standards. The question is, what makes us different from all those who fell to the illusion their relationships were above the rest? This morning, I tried to push away the notion of infatuation, on the premise I wasn't trusting the synchronous element of our union. But human logic, as faulty as it may be, and at the risk of demolishing the rhetorics of rewriting the past, is a powerful influence that seeks to attain balance by infusing elation with doubt. As much as I wish for us to be the real thing, I hear the voices of debate in the background, and I'm not sure which one of them is the one of wisdom," Patricia confessed.

"I would be a presumptuous fool to try to impress onto you that our relationship is backed by immutable, spiritual, and biological laws. Our rapport is as much defined by its length as it is by what it can achieve within that specific time period—be it seven days or longer. We may make elaborate plans one day, only to lose their meaning the next. We've seen it happen to others, and I'm sure we can find many examples within our respective lives, under various situations. Until purpose is clearly defined, it is nearly impossible to project the course of the future. But the tools for defining that purpose are not necessarily out of the reach of the focused and authentic mind. It's a matter of wanting it badly enough with a clear understanding of the implications."

"So, here's the question, John—do you want it badly enough?" she probed.

"Ignoring what I just said, and operating strictly at the gut level—yes."

"Now, John, suppose you could distill time into a single moment, bring everything that you have, the knowledge, the aspirations, the commitments and responsibilities to it—could you still honestly say it's what you badly wanted?"

"I'm at the center of my universe, Patricia—I mean what I say."

"Don't be offended if it sounds like a test, but I need to assuage some fears—if I told you I didn't hold the same feelings, would you still want a relationship with me?" she asked, nearly in tears.

"I'm old and wise enough to understand my sanity is contingent on harmony and a balanced emotional field. The answer is a clear no. If it were the case, I would consider my attraction to you purely lustful and devoid of meaning, which is something I would never allow at this point—I no longer do sex for sex's sake."

"So you would just return to England and forget about me?"

"It's hypothetical Patricia—I trust you didn't override your fears of men to fall into emotional disarray. If I didn't believe you wanted it badly enough yourself, we wouldn't presently be talking about this."

"So, you're not even going to ask the question?"

"You needed to ascertain where I stood in order to define your own position."

"So, you're mad at me?"

"No, not at all, I'm just going to wait for you to tell me without me asking."

"OK, I want it bad enough too!"

"*Shift* number three on the way!"

They both laughed before pulling each other close for a long kiss. Behind them, the Golden Gate Bridge and the Marin Headlands were basking in the orange glow of a magnificent sunset.

— o —

That night, Patricia stayed at the Fairmont. She forgot, or no longer cared, about what she had said concerning the sterility of hotel rooms. Everything was tinted by the hues of a new inner landscape. She had come to recognize what she had been silently waiting for all of her adult life—a union that would see to the expansion of her soul, whether through kindness and perseverance or the fearless drive to explore the unknown as one. She imagined the two of them as two eagles soaring above the heights of their reality, overseeing its fundamental makings with the keen eyes of sated hunters, peacefully assessing the options that lay ahead, forcing nothing, just letting the thermal currents do the work— without and within. They had made love once more. And though, she and John were lying side by side, she felt him inside her, as if he were to remain there indefinitely. Perhaps, he too sensed he was still there...

"Are we one, John," she asked.

"It does feel that way, doesn't it?"

"Not so long ago, it would have scared me."

"True intimacy requires courage, the courage to trust when trust calls."

"Something I could have written in my books."

"I have wondered lately about the possibility of a

73

shared spatial environment, and the nature of consciousness within it—an environment capable of storing memory and forming the equivalent of an easily accessible neurological matrix."

"It means two or more people could access the same information. It would then just be a matter of who's willing to add to the pool for all to share. I imagine that would require strong shields, or, unmitigated trust," she pondered.

"You just said it—trust again. On the other hand, shields might prove limiting to the process of sharing."

"Imagine a world without shields..." she mused.

"It's a hard sell, but it only takes two willing souls to get it started—two birds flying above a common land."

"Two birds, hey?"

"It sort of made itself up," he humored.

"I think I'm already liking your theory, John."

— o —

Patricia awakened within the dream—a familiar recurring pattern whose memories were usually gone by morning, or in the process of quickly fading into a fog that blurred the lines between the real and the imagined. For now, all had the appearance to solidity. In fact, her surroundings sparkled of a brilliance rarely seen in the waking state. She accepted she was dreaming and that her body was asleep somewhere. She didn't care where—it didn't matter. All that mattered was that she remembered the vitality of her experience upon the return of her consciousness to that body.

She and John were in a car. He drove. She touched the dashboard to ascertain its physics. She put her hand on her bare leg to trigger a sense-based response—her fingers and thigh registered signals on contact. She turned to John—he was smiling.

"You're aware it's a dream, aren't you?" he said.

"I have noticed."

The rental wasn't the Chevy Bolt, but another model. It didn't really matter what model, but what mattered was that they were driving on the same stretch of road they had traveled the other day, between Stinson Beach and Point Reyes Station—in a different car. It meant it wasn't the same event.

"We are returning to Drake's Beach, aren't we?" she asked.

"It was your idea, Patricia."

Patricia couldn't remember making that choice. Actually, she couldn't remember anything prior to finding herself awake in the front passenger seat.

"When did you become aware of this, I mean, aware you were dreaming?" she asked.

"Oddly, I don't remember anything before it, but I'm fairly sure we were on the Golden Gate Bridge, leaving San Francisco."

"I don't know about you, but I have a strange feeling about this, though it's not necessarily bad."

"As in momentarily eavesdropping on someone else's experience?"

"You've got it! I assume there have to be reasons for it."

"I guess the third *shift* comes with a special bonus assignment," he returned, offering a smile.

"Glad you brought your sense of humor with you. But tell me; how do you know I chose to go to Drake's Beach if you don't remember anything before the bridge.

I must have expressed that wish before we left the city?"

"I have no idea where the memory comes from—I just know it was your choice."

"Even though you didn't hear me mention it?"

"In you asking, it somehow connected to the appropriate memory."

"By appropriate, I suppose you mean one that is pivotal to us landing here, right?"

"I don't mean it as much as it is integral to the dominant experience. Aside from finding myself in this car ahead of you, I am in exactly the same state of bewilderment as you are. I advise we focus on the now and forego the origin of the dream, which probably belongs to the parts of us that have accepted this reality as their primary one," John answered.

"So, this is not just a dream, but a peek into a parallel existence, if I follow the logic."

"You either know it, or you don't, but yes, it appears so—which brings a whole new definition to our waking state notion of the dream world."

"Which day is it, John?"

"Hard to tell, but it can't be the same as the one of our sleeping bodies."

"Could it be another version of the trip we made to Point Reyes?"

"The one in which you made that choice instead of me? Can that even be plausible?" he pointed.

"I guess not—so it's got to be a different time. It has the feel of a Sunday or a holiday, gauging by the number of cars on the Shoreline," Patricia assessed.

"The next holiday is Wednesday—Administrative Professionals Day, you call it—two days before my planned return to the UK."

"Not much of a holiday, but enough of an excuse to take the day off for those who can," she remarked.

"A mere technicality."

"So then, this is our goodbye trip, John?"

"Which would explain why you chose the beach—it's a beautiful afternoon for love-making in the sand. Mind you, we may not enjoy the kind of privacy we had last time."

"So, we'll be caught nude in a dream—that wouldn't be the first time," she returned, laughing.

"I don't think this one is that kind of dream."

"The only thing that makes it different is the fact we are conscious inside it, as opposed to confused outside of it. We might not remember this the way we are presently experiencing it—just the part about being nude in public, if we get that far, say, and no memory of where we left our clothes," Patricia humored. "It might make it easier for us to remember if we tried our very best to bring what's happening to us now back to our waking selves—think of it as an exercise, John. We couldn't possibly be here if it wasn't important. We know, deep down, it's pivotal to the third *shift*—we've got to give it all we have!"

"It is clear that, right now, we're borrowing a window into a future or alternate version of ourselves. I don't believe these two are aware of our intrusion; if they are, it's likely to be in the form of a feeling of omnipresence. We may be in their space, but we aren't altering their experience," John said.

It was all for Patricia's dream—its future entered the same darkness from which it had emerged. It belonged to another's reality, regardless of whether that someone was her or not. For now she and John were sleeping in the last embrace of their love-making. The morning would decide whether their wish to remember yielded a quivering strand of memory or that the dream would be forever lost, like the many before it, in which she had made the conscious effort of informing the waking self of the reality of other worlds out there—worlds just as vivid as the rising sun bouncing off the colors of her paintings around the room, as she sipped her first cup of coffee, while, ironically, trying to remember her dreams.

— o —

When John found himself in the driver's seat, halfway across the Golden Gate Bridge, Patricia was looking towards the bay.

"It's nice to see people sailing their boats in the middle of the week—it feels like a Sunday. I'm so glad we decided to take off for Marin, John—I will dearly miss you when you're gone."

John was confused—which reality was he in? Patricia felt like a different version of herself—and what did she mean by midweek? He blacked out only to reemerge later, in the same driver's seat, somewhere between Stinson Beach and Point Reyes Station. This time, he understood he was dreaming, mesmerized by finding himself focused. He looked at his passenger.

"You're aware it's a dream, aren't you?"

"I have noticed."

He and Patricia had agreed they were on their way to Drake's Beach, piggy-backing the experience of future, and potentially, alternate versions of themselves. But shortly after they made the conscious choice of remembering the experience, Patricia left the dream to be replaced by the proper self of that reality.

"I wish we had found a quick fix to our dilemma, John, but I understand you must go back to sort things out. I will be staying put until I hear from you—I don't want to lose you, my dear man," she said.

John suddenly felt he didn't belong—just like on the bridge. It was time for his consciousness to return to its rightful place. He was gone in an instant.

5 – THE FIFTH DAY

Patricia was first to wake up. It was a quiet Saturday morning outside the Fairmont; but inside, there was a continuous movement of customers checking out of their rooms. For many of the medical professionals who had visited the convention, it was time to return to their lives, some as far as Japan, South Africa, and Australia. She got up to use the bathroom, still half asleep, but it wasn't until she sat on the toilet that she recalled some of the crazy dream she had. The memory was far from clear, but she distinctly remembered being aware of her own presence in it. That revelation was enough to uncover the greater details. She walked out of the room, naked, in search of pen and paper to write down her thoughts before they left her for good. She needed an anchor—it was too important. There was a message she needed to decipher, but the finer details were nothing but a blur. In the dream, John also knew where he was. They were driving somewhere, somewhere in Marin—many cars, the feel of a weekend, maybe a holiday. John was leaving soon for England—it was next week. They were on their way to Drake's Beach—naked bodies, lost clothing—laughter— her own laughter.

The dream wasn't what she was accustomed to— it was too powerful, too un-dream-like. She looked at herself in the full-length mirror, as if to verify she was seeing the right person. She wondered if John had really been there, at the wheel of the vehicle taking them back to the place where they had made love for the first time. The sensation of having eavesdropped on someone else's life was unsettling, yet it was her life she had peeked into. How could there have been two of herself? Her brain was aching under the strain, unable to make the data coalesce into a singular picture—too many obscure elements striving to overlap, forcing a momentary freeze-over. She wanted to believe there was a message that needed decrypting, yet the information bottlenecked at the gates of awareness. She waited for John to wake up.

— o —

John's iPhone buzzed at seven. He picked it up, shut the alarm off, and checked the screen for messages, before he realized Patricia was looking at him from across the room.

"Did you sleep well?" he asked.

"Yeah, except for some wild dreams."

"Feel free to share, I had a puzzling one of my own."

"You go first, John."

"Nothing much, but it sort of freaked me out. I was driving with you on the Golden Gate Bridge, save that you were a different you. I totally felt out of place, as if I had been in the wrong body. It was utterly vivid though—that was the odd thing—like I was visiting some variance of reality—a different time. Now, I remember, you said it felt like a Sunday, though it was the middle of the week—lots of boats on the bay..."

"Administrative Professionals Day?"

"How do you know?"

"You said I was there."

"In my dream?"

"Well, yeah, wasn't I sitting next to you?"

"You remember being there?" he asked, befuddled.

"I remember being there later when we were driving on Highway 1."

"Wait a sec... Drake's Beach—we were on our way to Point Reyes!"

"That was when you and I realized we were in a dream, or rather, witnessing a future event. You do recall being aware of your environment, right?"

"I remember making sure the steering wheel was solid, if that is what you mean. So, yes, I was aware."

"And you were aware I was too?"

"Well, it's a bit foggy, but I don't see why you wouldn't have been—the whole thing felt real. Actually, that explains why I didn't feel out of place on that stretch, because now I recollect that when you left, things got odd again—like you had resumed with being the other you. So, now you are actually saying you had the same dream...?" he queried, bemused.

"It would appear so, John; but I don't think it was a dream per se—or perhaps that's what all dreams are when we wake up in them. It was more like we were visiting an event that had not yet happened. You said it was my wish to go back to Drake's Beach. So now, I'm at a loss for words, since how would I not want to go back there, if only to see how it will turn out?" Patricia replied.

"Who wouldn't want to know? The question remains; would you wish to go back there even if you hadn't had the dream, Patricia?"

"Of course, I would love to; especially knowing you'll be gone soon. Making love on that beach again would be so totally perfect."

"So, that is what we'll do. On Wednesday, we go to Marin—any reservations?" he offered.

"There is something set in it that I find perplexing, as if it belonged to memory before it actually happened."

"Well, it did happen, but in the future instead of the past."

"Wow, my poor head, but the question remains of whether it is truly a set-thing or not. Are we possibly looking at one specific outcome among other possibilities; meaning there could be multiple versions of that trip? And what is the message?" she asked.

"That's why there are three more days before it happens, so that we get a chance at figuring it out. Things will eventually make sense."

"I'm glad we were able to retain the essence of it though—the dream, that is. I think we did well. Now, what about some breakfast, John?"

— o —

Patricia and John sat at the communal table of *Home : Table*, a stone's throw from the hotel. Saturday morning wasn't the easiest time for a breakfast of organic fares, since most places closed for the weekend. But it was early enough for the tiny eatery to offer a modicum of comfort, notwithstanding the coffee was great and the food excellent.

"I am scheduled to meet with colleagues from nine-thirty till noon. After that, I'm free for the rest of the day. Do you have plans of your own, Patricia?"

"It's funny, John, most people would have by now been informed of each other's schedules, but we're so caught up talking about existential stuff that we miss on all the fun," she humored with pointed delight.

"I know—while we're together, we aren't so good

with the things we would normally be doing. I have had a hard time focusing on my profession, but on the other hand, it's not everyday that one finds himself in the company of greatness."

"Thank you, same here, sweet man—I should be thinking about my next work shift, but it feels like eons away. I actually don't care, which is unusual for me. Go with the flow; that's what I say!"

"So, OK to meet after my mini-conference?"

"Let's take a long walk in Golden Gate Park, it looks like it's gonna be another beautiful day. What about getting together at two by the carousel, you know where that is? It will give me the opportunity to tidy a few things up, including taking a warm bath," Patricia proposed.

"It's been a while since I've been there, but I'll find it."

"I'm sure you will—you studied within a short distance of it. Don't tell me you never took a girl to the park," she teased.

"You would be amazed!"

— o —

Twenty-five years prior, John had actually taken a girl to the very spot from which he was observing parents letting their kids loose on the sandy area of the playground. He couldn't remember her name, not that it mattered, but he had hoped she liked him as much as he thought he did her. It turned out that she was only interested in having him help with her studies, a short con she had hoped would have excluded sex between them. But she wasn't any smarter at it than she was with her texts. It became immediately evident she navigated solo on choppy waters, unaware of the flimsy set painted by her poorly written script. It made John smile. How indubitably extreme that situation had been in regard to his relationship with Patricia. It was the fake versus the real, a vacuous zone against substance. The world was a stage full of bad actors, yet he recognized that by not validating their roles, he was dangerously flirting with nihilism. Wasn't it best to presume they genuinely acted their parts, and that projection was instead the deceiver, the inauthentic critic preaching from his high moral grounds? The blunt of the irony was well deserved, he thought, just as Patricia was seen walking towards him, waiving and smiling.

"Hello, John, how was your meeting?"

"It turned out well—nice to see old friends in the flesh as opposed to Skyping. And how was your bath?"

"Long, extremely relaxing, and generously bubbly—plus the sun was shining through the stained glass hanging, turning the bathroom into a temple. It was the perfect environment for recapping the dream."

"Any new thoughts about it?"

"Mostly, I was trying to figure out the reasons for it. Obviously, we didn't find ourselves in the same dream by accident. We spoke of a *third shift*, one that would put the two of us on a path between my life in San Francisco and yours in Britain. Maybe that trip to Point Reyes takes us to its gates, to something we haven't thought about, because what's missing belongs to the future. Since there was nothing ominous about the dream, I don't believe it is trying to warn us—which doesn't mean I didn't think about it for a second," she explained.

"I agree there was nothing portentous, since essentially, we were the dream. If it is at all related to the *shift* in question, then it is taking us to a marker, just as you said. I don't think the message is in trying to remember more of it, as opposed to understanding what we already have."

"Exactly what I was aiming at. The crux of it is that we barged on the two of us on our way to Drake's Beach on what appears to be next Wednesday. We could easily challenge that vision by opting out, but I don't think it's where we're at, since we have already agreed to go there. I don't recall we have a good reason to mess with what comes to assist us in solving the dilemma of our relationship. So, understanding why we chose to visit what may end up being a probability, is of crucial importance," Patricia voiced.

"I don't think I have a ready-answer for it at the moment—maybe that long walk in the park will spark the process. What do you say we get going?"

— o —

It wasn't an afternoon particularly bent on discussing the nature of existentialism. John first wanted to see the Conservatory of Flowers, while Patricia insisted they make sure to visit the De Young Museum and the Academy of Science. John opted for the Japanese Tea Garden; Patricia pushed for a stroll in the Botanical Garden. Then it was Stow Lake and Strawberry Hill, Spreckels Lake, the Polo Field... By the time they arrived at Queen Wilhemina Tulip Garden, near the Great Highway and Ocean Beach, they were ready to visit a different kind of garden—the Coastal Beer Garden, breaking their vow of sticking to organic, and settling for comfort food instead. They both refrained from the main attraction, staying alcohol-free under the set promise of their first meeting at the Top of the Mark.

"That was fun, John, now I'm ready for a nap."

"Just when I was about to propose we jog the whole way back?"

"Jog your heart out, doc, I'll catch a bus!" Patricia exclaimed with a laugh.

"What about we lie in the grass like all these fine people out there?"

"Now you're being nice, then we can dip our toes in the ocean after it!"

"Speaking of ocean, I was thinking of checking out the other beaches tomorrow—I never had a chance, or the motivation, to make it there on my other trips—any takers?" he proposed.

"The beauty of San Francisco is that besides Ocean Beach, and China Beach at Sea Cliff, most of the others are either nude beaches or part of them are. From Marshall's Beach, closest to the Golden Gate, to Baker Beach, and even tiny, secluded Mile Rock Beach below Lincoln Park, you can get a full tan, or in your case, a full burn," Patricia joked.

"A city after my own heart."

"Try that on the Cam River, John!" she bragged.

"It's River Cam for us English, and we do it with a proper picnic and shade umbrellas, as we lazily watch lovers in freshly pressed white garments row their boats—what civilized people do, Patricia."

"I hope you made that up—as lovely as it sounds and quaint as it may be, it feels painful."

"Not until a couple of drunken skinheads show up to break the spell with loud, uninvited remarks in incomprehensible English that may include, in no particular order: tits, bollocks, birds, cunt, piss off, balls up, bloke, daft, the list goes on, with ample infusions of the expletive *fuckin'* to hammer the point," he humored.

"About as subtle as fully-clothed perverts donning mirrored shades, checking dicks and pussies at Baker Beach," she countered.

"A class of its own, dear Patricia."

"All puns aside, it sounds like a lovely idea—though the beaches are going to be crowded on a sunny Sunday afternoon—warm and clear for another week, the weatherman says!"

"People like to bundle together, regardless of their claims to individualism—nothing wrong with joining a crowd!"

"From my perspective, John, I see people all day long, so I generally try to keep it quiet whenever I can."

"If it gets too wild, we can always try Mile Rock—you said it was secluded."

"It's a solid option—it's kind of a gay hangout, but it's not like it used to be in the eighties when it was mostly men—I've seen lots of women there lately."

"What about Marshall's—I have a feeling it might be manageable. That is one I researched in the day."

"Department of intuitions?"

"Yes, the brainiacs," he returned, laughing.

"One thing I love about you, John, is that you laugh readily and you are even-tempered—the stuff of trust."

"I've always been easy-going—not that it necessarily served me well when it came to women."

"What are the women you speak of, my good man? Surely, they can't be that wise."

"It was mostly in my youth—not enough danger for some of them."

"The character of the young—you don't want to know till it burns. It doesn't matter what mamma says."

"Sounds like you've been there..."

"I have. I believed I was tough, except danger was waiting for me instead of it just being my middle name. It could have been worse—like in some narrowly averted probability," she replied.

"Like the one before the *first shift* with the awful past?" he probed.

"You get the idea, John."

"I get the idea that your smarts probe depths rarely visited by the common mortal. How exactly did you figure out all the stuff that flies under the radar?"

"I was born with the gift of curiosity teamed to passion. Maybe we all come with it, but I chose to use it. That's why I could never accept bullshit growing up, which, naturally, led to clashes with parents and teachers alike, followed by rebellion and all the silly things that ensue when it is mixed with misguided certainty. But the undeniable principles of undaunted curiosity form the base of knowledge, and with enough drive, you end up finding yourself on a path seldom trodden. But it's also a lonely place. So, when I meet someone on it, it is bound to send waves to the far-reaching shores of my psyche. I know it's beyond your question, but that's the effect you have on me, John."

"You're actually saying that the quest for knowledge is a lonely road?"

"Isn't it what it looks like when you've passed all the official directional markers, when knowledge is no longer handed down, but mined from within the deep strata of the self? It's as if, at the last checkpoint, someone told you, 'Kiddo, you're on your own!' But the irony is, when you come back with what you've found, you realize that the mind that keeps a hold on accepted knowledge, is only interested in choking the new—as if the known had crystallized into something precious, immutable, and intolerant."

"What some call the calcification of knowledge—it's a common stigma in the scientific world, though, in general, you don't hear much about it."

"It's everywhere, like a cold hand that freezes everything it touches. It erodes common sense, eats at logic, turns brilliance into apathy—and I don't even know what to call it," Patricia voiced in disgust.

"We're back once again at trying to define what it is with the ego personality that is corrupt

. Is it something biological, or does it reside outside, in the global social framework, like a program, say—and why does it affect some more than the others?" John posed.

"From where I'm at, it appears to be tied to value—the value of the self over that of the collective; the compulsion to overtake, control, and annihilate what drives others to do the same—an alpha syndrome of sort that only highlights the ego's abdication of its powers while doing all it can to diminish and stifle what demonstrates the auto-implied superiority of what it fears, essentially, by denying knowledge to come forth. In other words, a mind fuck of epic proportions, considering that what the ego fears is essentially itself. As to the why, my dear man, I can only guess that it is to basically test its own limits."

"That would be assuming that the ego understood the notion of limits. But *limits* meaning what exactly—the point of no return, the apocalypse?"

"Look at it for what it is, John, it's not stopping—it won't stop until it comes to the gates of ultimate destruction. And if it's lucky, it'll get a whiff of what lies behind, and perchance, it will turn around before momentum takes it to its well-suited predicament. Just like a stubborn teenager that wants to see the world burn and goes on mowing his classmates with an assault rifle."

"A sinister picture, Patricia, but is it truly what you believe?"

"It's what I believe when I'm reminded that the bullshit that should have vanished millennia ago is still with us," she resigned herself to say.

"I thought *shift number one* took care of that," he casually reminded her.

"Oops, planets Faith and Trust to Patricia!"

"*Shift one* still active, checked!" he humored.

"Blame it on the greasy fries!"

"Try the malt vinegar next time."

Patricia rolled over to sit on John's lower section.

"I could fuck you right here and now, funny man," she warned playfully.

"I don't know how the natives would react—there have to be customs in these parts, dear."

"The natives you speak of are probably tourists from France—they won't mind."

"Not if they know I'm British—they're still mad about Joan of Arc."

"As they should be!"

"Before I devolve to the point of shaming my country, what about that toe-dipping in the brine offer?"

"OK then, you're free, mister!"

"It's hard to believe that beyond the windmill and that line of trees, the next significant landmass is Japan,"

John stated absentmindedly.

"Latitudinally perhaps, but I'm fairly certain Hawaii and Russia are closer," she argued.

"It's a metaphor for perspective, Patricia—the poetic mind cares little about accuracy."

"Spatial perspective is an elusive companion that only serves when the mind deals in blindness, for if all presents can exist as one, the same goes of places," she countered.

"So, you're essentially saying that Japan is directly behind that row of cypresses?"

"No, I'm saying that here and Japan share the same space."

"And you would know that from...?"

"Directly from the department of intuitions."

"No brainiacs involved, of course?"

"No, they would try to convince me that there's a whole ocean in between—that would be the work of the department of fossilized concepts."

"You have a way of fossilizing existence into what some may call denial of the facts."

"Are you probing or judging?"

"I too am a curious soul—judgment has no place in my life. I'm only interested in corroborating my own findings against, or rather, through what you know," John replied, worried he had given the wrong impression.

"And...?"

"It is becoming clear that for theoretical thinking to reach the realm of the factual, it must first garner confidence through the findings of others. With it, comes the desire to push the limits, to dare probing the depths of the intuitive in ways that turn old concepts on their heads. I have seldom found in others what you are willing to put on the proverbial table of discourse. I hope that clarifies where I stand. I understand that, on occasion, we lose our footing with trust, but I'm not going anywhere, Patricia. What exists between us belongs to the sacred—I will never betray it," he asserted.

"Same here, John, but I was just playing into that sense of humor of yours. I'm far from being upset. In fact, if I were, I would worry about myself—there is nothing in you, so far, that has ushered me towards reconsidering the soundness of our connection, and somehow, I trust I will never have to go there."

"Thank you—that means a lot."

They playfully pulled themselves away from the grass, and then started walking in the direction of the line of trees that stood between them and Japan.

— o —

"Tomorrow night's drumming night. I'd love to take you there, but it's girls only. I have to return to my place from the beach by six. It would be a good time to regroup mentally and emotionally, at least for me," Patricia said, as they walked barefoot in the wet sand, avoiding the occasional jellyfish.

"Perfect, I will be meeting the next day with neurosurgeons from UCSF, Davis, and Stanford. There is a strong possibility that I shall be traveling to Palo Alto as well. It would be a good time for me to prepare."

"I enjoy the feng shui of our relationship, John; there is a definite easiness of flow within it that makes for a strong argument for trust."

"Something that was missing with Jane, my wife of many years. We clashed about schedule at every opportunity. It was a case of bringing the worst out of each other, as part of irremediable reflexive patterns. It seemed that the more we tried to fix the issue, the bigger it became. In the end, there was nowhere left to go. From my present perspective, it was the best way for me to grow a spine. As I said, I have always been easy-going, but there is a fine line between that quality, and apathy as the result of emotional and mental fatigue. Jane is not to blame—no-one is. I simply must validate that time together for the lesson it provided—it being to never repeat. The years I have spent alone since then, have taught me to strengthen my resolve to find partners with a better awareness of themselves. Little did I know that it would take me so long—and here—to find one of them," John confessed, smiling at an understanding Patricia.

"It's also been quite a while since I broke up with my last girlfriend. It appears patterns develop regardless of sexual orientation. It's a people thing—look at brothers and sisters, and what we call tough love! There's nothing to romanticize about when dealing with the stifling of personal, evolutionary consciousness. As you just said, and I fully concur, we must take the time to gather our personal armies in order to be ready to fight the resurgence of bad habits—and I mean, until they're all vanquished," Patricia articulated.

"A potent metaphor for looking at the self from an honest stance. It's why a term like *being on the rebound* exists—timing is of the essence."

"And with proper timing come the best options—not to be confused with waiting indefinitely for something to happen while popping bonbons, if you get my drift."

"I get the drift of your colorfulness, Patricia, something that suits you well, if I may say so. But once more, we are assessing the necessity for an authentic look at change. It seems you and I are walking hand in hand into an agreeable situation, and I hope it includes a healthy alternative to living far apart."

"If we put our faith and resources into *shift number three*, I have no doubt such an alternative will emerge from unsuspected places. It might involve sacrificing a few of the things we deem important, even though they're not. It's amazing what we get attached to that does nothing but slow us down. Sentimentality, in spite of its noble side, can be an invisible tether. I used to never go out of town because of my cat—then one day, she was gone. Only later did I find that she had moved in with the neighbors. What does it say of attachment, John?"

"We do the same with houses, cars, the objects on the mantle—some of them with forgotten meaning, or reasons why we put them there in the first place. *Invisible tether* is a brilliant comparative—there's even a tarot card, the Devil, that illustrates the symbolic meaning of human bonding to material things, be they real or imagined."

"You must have fired the brainiacs at your department of intuitions—that, my dear man, is a sweet interpretation of the obvious, yet many so-called tarot readers are blind to it."

"I'm not into tarot but I've always liked the card. To me, the Original Sin analogy is indicative of its human origin. It illuminates what was said about the ego and how it operates through smoke and mirrors, the way it imagines its enemies, all the while being the prime mover—the architect."

"As much as there is written about the ego, the mind, or the spirit-in-body, as it is sometimes called, your views on its misplaced powers are fascinating. I don't recall ever coming across any writing or reading highlighting the paradox at which it sits in such basic and potent terms. I have my own views that don't differ much from yours, but you live at the heart of the corruption. I am led to believe you're not just working from a stream of consciousness," she praised.

"It's likely at the root of my interest in neurology. I have always been fascinated by what ticks the human psyche—the behind-the-scene items that keep us from evolving less chaotically. Most of our technological achievements have been around the war machine. The field of medicine at large has been dependent on creating better and healthier soldiers, while keeping on learning about the human body as we patched them up. There is inherent barbarism to it all, including the poison industry in charge of processing our food, the space program struggling to define its colonial footing, and the development of green technology out of necessity, as opposed to common sense. Instead of calling it bullshit, I opted for the quieter side of things by referring to it as *stigmatic behavior*," John explained.

"Even though history has been punctuated by eras of renaissance and other spurts of human brilliance, what I was referring to earlier as value of the self above others, has been weighing down on the chances of an evolutionary process without major conflicts, at least that's what it seems from ground zero," Patricia reasoned.

"Actually, it brings me to evaluate history from the standpoint of outer perspective instead of ground zero. I agree with you, but you know just as well as I do that there is something grossly missing in the story of humanity that leaves one to wonder for whom it may have been written. If we were to compare eras of unrest versus those of peace, we might be surprised. I believe we live an epoch of great perplexity as to our prospects of survival as a race. It could be that we are becoming more aware at the mass level, meaning, more conscious of our inadequacies, of the lacunes in the fiber of our social and global makeup; more self-aware of our mistakes, and less tolerant of those we pinpoint in others. We are also experiencing so much more diversity than our ancestors did, such as being exposed to other cultures within our native environment, as opposed to colonizing foreign land; forced out of our comfort zone by the necessity to expand in ways that were deemed unthinkable half a century ago. Most likely, we are better off than what the appearances suggest, or what the media is serving us—news heavy on negativity, that is," John extended.

"Little do we forget, dear man—I should know better! I'm normally the first one to highlight the discrepancy, but with you, I somehow lean towards exploring the areas of my own fears. It's amazing what we can preach that we conveniently omit to apply to ourselves. I am guilty of reflexivity, though to my credit, I don't normally delve into its layers for too long. It's just that we bounce off each other in ways that leave no stones unturned—it's quite remarkable, really!"

"The concept of synchronicity is heavily explored in motion pictures, mostly via extraction of relevant concepts in psychology, or taken directly out of science fiction writing—the director J.J. Abrams comes to mind as an advocate of meticulously orchestrated synchronistic events, and as an avid explorer of the theory of probabilities. But day to day existence is having a hard time catching up with *new thinking*—though that may be an erroneous description for something that might have been knocking at the door for who knows how long."

"Life's a paradox, John, regardless of where we turn. Oddly, it appears said life can't exist without that distinction."

"I believe the paradox in question emerges from the basic push and pull of extremes, or if you prefer, complements—the male and female in all things. The fascination with opposites leads to overlooking the balancing point. It explains why those who live in a state of innate understanding of the harmony intrinsic to perceived competing forces, are least likely to sermonize about right and wrong."

"A view shared by countless thinkers over the millennia, John."

"Yes, I don't own it, if that's what you mean," he replied, laughing.

"I was just enforcing your point. The knowledge and the understanding are there—they have always been there. The way I see it, we're born with them."

"So the question is, Patricia, at what point do we start losing the message? And if civilization were to be compared to individual reality, at what point in our evolution did we start drifting away from that fundamental knowledge? Certainly, some of the Greek philosophers were onto something—after all, we're still learning from them."

"I guess, they came from the future."

Of course, they didn't, at least, not in layman terms, John thought, but the concept of overlapping presents made perfect sense at that very moment. Was knowledge the byproduct of the evolutionary process, or was evolution the means by which to access its infinity?

A case in which knowledge wasn't a function of time, and evolution was merely the linear component of a much more sophisticated system of adapting through the extraction of available knowledge.

"It feels good to walk on wet sand," Patricia said, as she wrapped her arm around John's waist.

6 – THE SIXTH DAY

Patricia and John had parked their rental in the crowded lot above Drake's Beach. As predicted, they would not benefit from the kind of intimacy they had enjoyed on their first visit. But Patricia figured that if they hiked deep enough, they would eventually see a significant thinning of users, and perchance, find privacy for the ritual of love-making. But just as she was about to answer John's question about bringing water, she was abruptly overtaken by a surge of anxiety about the normalcy of the moment—a normalcy that belonged to another time, another Patricia. She awoke to the realization that her experience was a continuation of the dream in which she had previously found herself by John's side, driving along Shoreline Highway out of Stinson Beach, except this time, John, the dreaming John, was absent. As much as she had been comforted by his presence, aware of exploring together in the previous encounter; finding herself alone this time around, brought forth apprehension that bordered on a sensation of spiraling into alienation. She feared she could end up being trapped in the wrong place and time, unable to find her bearings upon awakening in her regular world. John, the man she admired and loved so dearly, was nothing more than a stranger in the clutches of an affair with a different her. For a second, if she could call it that, she thought of the gap in time, or even stranger, the rip in the fabric of reality, as human consciousness understood it. There were roadways, hidden paths that veered off the consensed-upon highways of existence, that cared little for the manufactured laws of the established. There was comfort in accepting the alienness of her dream reality, as if her anxiety could be justified by surrendering, and soothed by the harvesting of new information. Rather than fighting her predicament, she opted to take advantage of her position, to access the deeper meanings of her experience, and perhaps, find what it was in *shift number three* that required of her and John to investigate in unusual places. But why hadn't he joined her—and where had he gone? She heard herself answer the question, "Yeah, let's bring water—I'm sure I'll want some after sex." She then felt the laughter coming out of a mouth that wasn't hers—yet, hers all the same—as sweet John cracked one of his smart ripostes. It was them alright, she thought, not just an abstraction fabricated by an overly imaginative mind. She soon figured out how to be both the observer and the subject, and also realized that the same could be applied to the reality whence she came. That was important. It was the knowledge she and John had breached upon during their last walk at Ocean Beach—the universal, ever-present pool that could be accessed from any point in time. The dream state was the road to it. It was all there, tucked in the folds of experience, ready to be picked upon reaching ripeness—a state dependent on the readiness of the self to accept the new as the inevitable transformation of the old, to trust that effervescent knowledge was ready to be tapped upon the mind's awaking. It was also a thought that brought forth the understanding that the development of cognitive abilities weren't insomuch a function of time as they were of the willingness to look for answers in unusual places— such as it was the case with her eavesdropping on the present of another time. The notion of rules had taken on the ethereality of a widening space between artifacts that only loosely connected to satisfy the exigencies of temporary functions. It all seemed unnecessary. There were few rules in the dream state, and they went by another name: *adaptive guidelines*—mostly to protect the traveler from inadvertently losing the thread of their search. She was such a traveler, but she hadn't been able to precisely define the nature of her quest—at least, not yet. It was more like what she was looking for was instead looking for her. But it made no difference—there was an undeniable magnetic reality to it that was in no need of concerning itself with primary polarization.

So, when John said, "My enquiry about the possibility of relocating to the area with my UCSF, Davis, and Stanford colleagues on Monday was received with lukewarm enthusiasm. It's an extremely competitive field, rife with ultra-qualified candidates—though they readily agreed that my contribution as a lecturer would be appreciated," she, the observer, got wind of complications ahead. But Patricia already knew that there were obstacles on both sides—the point was to find a common ground, something neither of them had yet been capable of coming up with. But then, what were the reasons to be looking for hints in a future event, so that they could be brought back to its relative past? What, in that past, was capable of shedding light on a detail that could just as easily have found its own sun in its proper space? Were those hints hidden in the stretching between the two time points? And what about the fact that distance was steadily diminishing to return to its legitimate geometric oneness? And then it came to her; what if *shift number three* couldn't unlock the dilemma of their position—what then? It meant that fundamental roadblocks were at stake, and that removing them would require such massive adjustments on both parts, that the task would be deemed insurmountable, leading to the abandonment of the hope of ending up together. She looked at the prospect with neutral resignation. She was in no position to evaluate her perception from the perspective of the observer—its intellectual and emotional qualitative was now in the hands of other Johns and Patricias, she had become the messenger, a state of being that straddled both realities—she had fully detached.

— o —

When Patricia woke up, she wished John had been by her side. He had returned to the hotel after they went out to the movies following their walks in the park and Ocean Beach. Even though he had invited her, she didn't feel the sterility of the room was in step with the uneven shapes of the day, the trees, the splashing of the waves, the windings paths... Her place was far more in line with that outside reality. She could have asked John to join her, but she didn't want to appear needy—a move she regretted for having been one of inauthenticity. She intuited he wouldn't want to impose; and thus, she didn't feel surprised when he kissed her goodbye and stayed on the N-Judah, on his way to Powell to catch the cable car to California. Perhaps he too hadn't been authentic with his feelings, but there were times when the human mind didn't quite align with the heart, as if some nondescript, minor forces softly clashed into a hazy sense of falseness. It was an adequate explanation for John not showing up in the dream, but she didn't buy it for long—that would have been reading into something that wasn't there. She took it that she had been meant to be alone to face her own doubts about their chances to find that middle ground. She had no difficulties recollecting the experience—the message was crystal clear. There were indeed insurmountable obstacles before them—her own unwillingness to contemplate moving out of San Francisco was one of them. Surely, she couldn't expect John to abandon his lifestyle, his friends, family, and successful career for a woman he had only known for a few days. It didn't matter how strong their connection was, it was only a diminutive week hopelessly tugging the whole of time against the flow. Either of them moving to join the other would suffer a diminishment in stature, a weakening of the foundation that supported their edifice, a devaluation of the self—unless, of course, such a move was in the form of a victory—a victory over adversity. She liked the thought—it had a reassuring ring to it. Surely, there were ways to win impossible battles—the human imagination was full of stories of victors against impossible odds, tales of resilience driven by the unshakable faith that a figment of godly justice would eventually prevail. She allowed the thought to die in the misery of its irrelevance. There were no battles, no boxing rings, no heroes—she probably was hallucinating. "Go back to sleep, Patricia," she said aloud.

— o —

John got up with the uneasy feeling something had slipped from under his feet. Why had he not asked if it was OK to spend the night with Patricia in her apartment after she declined his offer to stay at the hotel? She hadn't given the impression of wanting to be alone. But then she didn't offer either. He disliked the haze of the situation—there was an aura of incertitude about it that betrayed a slight misalignment of energies around their union. He had been there before, nearing the confluence of two rivers, rafting down the weaker waters, as he felt the stronger currents ahead drawing him towards the rapids. He sensed there was trouble with *shift number three*. From his perspective, it showed in the slight fraying of confidence around what lay before him. He felt the urge to grab his phone, but an inner voice called for caution—it was better that Patricia reached him first, was it not? He realized he was losing grip on his reality, giving in to inner struggle that most likely was in the form of old patterns refusing to make room for the joy of rebirth. He straightened his mental spine, finding renewed strength in affirming his intentions to be by Patricia's side, going down those rapids, instead of pulling into the safety of an eddy and abdicating his solemn promise. He picked up his iPhone just as it rang.

"Good morning, Patricia, I was just about to call—did you sleep well?"

"Hi, John—I did, but I had a rough ride halfway through the night. I'm sorry I didn't ask you to stay at my place—I could have used your warm body next to me."

"Do you care sharing?"

"I prefer to look in your eyes when I do. What about you meet me here—I'll have coffee and pancakes ready when you arrive."

"I'll call a cab as soon as I freshen up—I'll be there shortly!"

"You know, you're welcome to take a shower at my place—I miss you."

"I miss you too," he said softly.

Patricia ground coffee and started on the pancake batter. She felt relieved that John was his old self, and not the disconnected one of the dream. She reckoned that having returned from a strange place, gathered data from across the membrane of time, confused yet informed of some inner workings, had brought new light into her personal reality. She needed to hone her resolve and trust that whatever it was *shift number three* had in store was the better alternative. She also had to count on John sharing the same predicament and wishes. Together, they would overcome the hurdles and foray straight ahead.

— o —

John arrived forty-five minutes later with fresh squeezed organic orange juice he had picked up at Rainbow Grocery on his way.

"Best place by far—it's where I do all of my food shopping and more. How did you know about it?" Patricia asked as she kissed John.

"They were around when I studied at UCSF, though at a different location. I heard they started in the mid-seventies, ahead of a few other collectives. One of them was the Inner Sunset Community Food Store, where I did most of my shopping, since it was near the university and I lived close by."

"Yeah, I heard they tanked in the nineties. They were quite successful before the core of their original people moved onto other projects—at which point things started to spiral downwards. According to someone who used to work there, it appeared the new generation missed pathetically on the message. There were also rumors of internal wrongdoing, such as daily theft straight out of the

106

registers. More than you need to know, I'm sure."

"Petty crime is not my area of expertise, but from the standpoint of the overall picture, the information is relevant, especially since I knew the place quite well and I caught Chris Isaak shopping there one afternoon," he returned, laughing.

"Yeah, Twin Peaks was barely a mile or two from there," she jested.

They started on the pancakes.

"So, Patricia, do you want to talk about your rough stretch, last night?"

"Yeah, I had another one of those crazy dreams in which I was aware. Same thing as last time, except we had reached Drake's Beach, but you weren't with me, at least, not the present you, as in the first time."

"Are you sure I wasn't there?"

"Well, of course you were, but not in the sense of eavesdropping on a future you—you were the future you."

"So, in other words, you were investigating by yourself; do I get this right?"

"Kind of—it's hard to put into thoughts, never mind words," she answered hesitantly.

"So, what was rough about it?"

"You not being there was part of it. Me feeling I was caught in between two versions of my own, defying the time/space continuum, was, to say the least, a bit alienating. But when I heard you say that it would be extremely difficult for you to find a position in the area aside from lecturing, I realized we were in trouble. Not that I was alarmed then, but I knew that the information would affect the sleeping me upon awakening—and it did," Patricia explained.

"What were the circumstances around me knowing that it would be difficult to find a post in neurology?"

"Your meeting with your colleagues tomorrow."

John sat silent for a moment, while taking a sip out of his coffee.

"Nice brew by the way," he resumed. "That's quite the revelation, Patricia, but sincerely, I know it's going to be the case—it's a shot in the dark and I've been in this business long enough to be aware of the fierce competition I am facing. Plus, I'm fifty-two, which in some circles qualifies as ancient."

"So, it doesn't really worry you?"

"Of course it does—I mean, what kind of alternative am I left with? Something extraordinary needs to happen before things start making sense. But so far, I have refrained from rationalizing. I guess we are now facing a different kind of music, aren't we?" he admitted.

"So, you get what I mean by rough."

"But you must have also known, so, what is it that is making the difference?"

"Perhaps hearing it for the first time coming out of your mouth was what woke me up to it."

"We have to get to the bottom of what this actually means. From my standpoint it has all the looks of preparing us for the challenge ahead. Surely, the two of us riding in that car are not aware of what we presently know, yet, when we get to that point on Wednesday, it will be with this added knowledge. Those two are not the same us, they belong to a probability, unaware of the fact they had visitors," John put forth.

"Could it be that they aren't going through *shift three*, or that something is not allowing for it to coalesce, or even, that there are, as we briefly posited, more than one version of it?"

"Apparently, we are on a different course from them—your guess is as good as mine as to the variables. My overall feeling, from personal experience with the dream, tells of semi-detachment on their part, as if their commitment to the union were slightly askance from ours—a form of silent surrendering to the possibility of things not working out, if you know what I mean."

"So, you are saying they are doubtful of their prospect without really admitting to it?"

"Maybe they just don't know. Remember, they are who we were before the first dream."

"I am to conclude they never had these dreams, or if they did, they never remembered. So, what made the difference?"

"It must have been subtle—something that could have happened anywhere along the line of our short relationship. It probably doesn't matter at this time what or when it was," John returned.

"Yeah, it's fascinating in some quasi-scary way, but I agree—no point chasing the inconsequential."

"How do we go from here, Patricia? How do you see us surmounting the challenges that lie ahead?"

"Well, for one thing, what came out of the dream is obvious; the other two of us didn't apparently address the issue before your John, upon getting to Drake's Beach, spoke of his meeting with his colleagues. That gives us a three day edge over them. That is to me the reassuring part of being where we're at. We need to work as a team, explore our fears together and not let go of each other's hand—that is what I think is the fundamental difference between them and us. Whatever the reasons for it, I would much rather be here than there, though I understand that by fundamental, that difference might just as well be minute. I mean, it was, or is, invisible to them. It's hard to talk about the future in past terms. I assume their present is overlapping ours. The thing is, John, and in regard to what we breached in other discussions, those two courses are very close to each other, and thus could easily merge—meaning that we can't lose tract of the original intention behind *shift number three* if we're truly serious about the concept. And that's how I see it, John!"

"I didn't expect less of you, Patricia. What's mesmerizing about the two courses is the seemingly infinitesimal difference between them, as you so accurately pointed; yet, it's evident that we are rewriting the past in some fashion, but obviously not in a linear way, if that makes any sense."

"Which could also explain that in spite of heading in the same direction, our respective destinations might end up being quite dissimilar," Patricia added.

"So, rule number one: we stick together—what's number two?"

"We stick together some more, which means, no hiding, no lies, no doubts, and no escapist act—in other words: total support. Can you live with that, John?"

"I can, as long as by escapist act you mean running away from doubt and fear."

"I see your point. By *no doubts*, I meant trust in each other."

"All good then—what about you; can you live by your own rules?"

"I trust myself from the bottom up—I walk my talk. You can count on that, John!"

110

"Then we have a formidable deal. In my opinion, it is far better than conventional marriage."

"You got that right, mister—no bullshit!"

They laughed, knowing that whatever would stand before them would be nothing more than loose elements of fear—the rest would simply be manageable.

— o —

The yellow cab dropped Patricia and John at the top of the Marshall's Beach trail. The part nearest the parking lot was packed, but the lower half was nearly deserted, at the exception of scattered nudists along its narrow length. It was perfect. They took their clothes off and lay on the towels provided by Patricia. The Golden Gate Bridge looked imposing from left of below. A container ship on its way to Asia appeared dwarfed by the colossal structure.

"An exceptional day by San Francisco standards—I wonder what happened to the rain you brought with you from Britain?" Patricia teased.

"A strong Mexican wind pushed the clouds away, I was told."

"I have a particular fondness for wise weathermen—perhaps you can put me in touch with him?"

"It's a she."

"Damn, just when I'm starting to like guys again, you throw a girl at me!"

"Life loves a good pendulum."

"Watch out, or you'll end up swinging with the fish," she humored, putting on a deep Mafioso accent.

John couldn't help bursting into laughter.

It was all about the timing, Patricia's face, her naked breasts, reshaped and inviting as she lay on her side, the words that came out of her mouth, so surprisingly low and in a nearly perfect Italian accent—it was so deliciously unreal. John couldn't contain himself—this woman wasn't only physically irresistible, she was witty beyond belief. "What an extraordinary person!" he thought.

"You're something else, Patricia!"

"And I love you too, John," she bounced, with a mischievous sparkle in her eye.

"If you keep on looking at me this way, I'm going to settle for a janitorial position at the bus terminal. Cambridge begone!"

"Problem solved—next!"

"I love you, Patricia."

"Finally, what took you so long?!" she playacted.

"I had to break the barrier—it's done."

"Now, I really want to make love."

"Have mercy—not here!"

"I'm totally wet and I can tell you have an erection under there," she said, as she fished for John's penis between his belly and the towel.

"You're not serious—you're going to have us arrested!"

"Alright then, but we're leaving early for my place—deal?"

"How can I refuse?!" he uttered, deliriously vanquished.

Patricia got up and ran to the waves. She dove in the frigid waters as if they had been the turquoise of the Bay of California, down in Mexico. John quickly followed, anxious to cool the heat that had overtaken his body. There was no seething; rather, the sensation of having been dipped in ice water enveloped him. Patricia laughed.

"That took it right out of you, hey, John?!"

She was impervious to the brine's low temperature—a mermaid in her natural element came to John's mind.

"How come you don't feel it?!"

"I feel it, but I don't let it overwhelm me!" she shouted over the crash of the waves.

"Is that what you call mind over body?!"

"It's what I call a marriage of mind and body, John!"

"Any particular trick to it?!"

"Trust—the trust that the body can take care of itself!"

"What about the dictates of biology and physics?!"

"What about them, John, aren't they just in your mind? I don't see any tablets on this beach, itemizing the cause and effect of our actions!"

"You're taking it into abstract territory—there's no such thing as being above natural laws. It's verified science, Patricia!"

"As observed by the eye that wants to see!" she taunted.

"Am I being tested?!"

"Yes, you are, doc!"

The line between seriousness and humor was indeed blurred by Patricia's unabashedness to cross it without so much as making it a relevant marker. Life couldn't be serious in the light of its mix of playfulness and absurdity. At least, that was what she was thinking as she baited John about the rigidity of some of his views. Of course, she knew certain laws couldn't easily be broken, that her body couldn't sustain itself through a long exposure to waters that had taken so many to the dark side of hypothermia, but she also intuited that a lot of man's weaknesses resided in faulty assumptions about the body and the self at large. That was what she meant by marriage of body and mind, as opposed to the subjugation of the body by the mind. She thought of it as a ridiculous item of insolence on the part of rational thinking to conclude the mind could dominate the body, when, as she saw it, the mind was merely aligning itself with the built-in resilience of that body—a body far quicker at responding to its environment than the mind was, and far more adapted to it, for it was part of it. The environment was its extension—its cocoon. What made that cocoon warm or cold, comfortable versus not, had a lot to do with how the mind perceived that environment, and to some extent, manufactured it into a sensory reality. Of course, that went against the grain of just about everything, but she didn't care. She didn't care because she didn't live anyone else's life but her own, and in her life rules were different—she was in charge of making them and breaking them.

John had never met a person that was so tuned in to her personal reality as Patricia was. She was forcing him to look at his own, from a standpoint very unlike what he was now referring to as the easy chair of self-evaluation. There was no place to comfortably settle in when the work was constant, when it entailed a relentless examination of unchallenged beliefs tied to monstrously distorted assumptions about the mechanics of life, within and without the self. She challenged the foundation of his teaching, but not necessarily to the point of weakening it inasmuch as she was providing structural components to its reinforcement. She was a hard sell to his field, but science could no longer deny the vitality of the subjects it had conveniently ignored for so long. There were no miracles to decry when there was an extraordinary world to embrace. His field was, to a point, guilty of pessimism and hypocrisy, but he didn't feel it was the solution to alienate it by pinpointing its faults—the fix lay in patience and the trust that, eventually, universal understanding would impregnate the cloth of acquired knowledge.

— o —

Finally, Patricia came out of the water. Her skin had taken on the looks of a three-dimensional landscape of goose bumps, and her hard, erect nipples were playing tricks on John's mind.

"You look insanely beautiful," he advanced.

"Beauty is in the eye of the beholder. Obviously, you haven't paid attention—one of my breasts hangs lower than the other, my labia is asymmetrical, and when I squeeze my butt, the cellulite thinks it's time to go on a parade. But thanks anyway!"

"I wasn't aware you were so hard on yourself. Of course I didn't see any of that, probably because it's all in your head," he returned.

"Us girls have our insecurities, but overall I like what I see when I look at myself in the mirror—I would date that woman in a heartbeat."

"I prefer the sound of that, but I hope you're not insinuating guys don't have hang-ups," he tested.

"Oh, get real, John, I wasn't comparing. I mean, what's the scoop with dick size and all that shit? I've never met a girl who cared, unless she was an idiot."

"Don't ask me; I wouldn't know. But I'm aware it's out there, and how it affects some individuals."

"Like the president?"

"I would have to be his personal physician to answer the question, but I'm cognizant of the rumors."

"Some say Hitler had a micro-penis, which they claim was tied to the horrific acts he was responsible for."

"I guess it makes the point of the shit you are referring to—these claims are its incontrovertible proof. I don't think the field of psychology necessarily agrees with these people's insinuations. There is no substance of direct relation between penis size and evil—it's simply preposterous."

"So, in essence, you're denying the reality of overcompensating, right?"

"We overcompensate for many reasons. I'm not saying insecurities tied to physiognomy aren't real, just that they don't provide the whole picture on stigmatic human behavior."

"Just curious—I agree. I suspected you had some angle on it."

"It all ties, once again, into what we talked about previously: the near-perverse deviance of the ego from its spiritual counterpart."

"A separation that essentially leads to losing common sense and opening the gates of insanity."

"In a nutshell, yes."

"What else can we disagree about?" she poked, laughing.

"We aren't good for each other," he replied.

"Control to team—abort *shift three*!" she exclaimed.

"All arousals disabled!" he followed.

They looked at each other, breaking into laughter. They were two adults who had found their inner child and were running away with it. How sublime it was to be reborn into an earlier time with the wisdom of age!

— o —

The pair raided the Rainbow Grocery deli on their way back to Patricia's apartment from Marshall's Beach. After showering, they ate, and then pondered on a choice of tea out of Patricia's large selection. Drum practice wasn't for another two hours, so they sat on the patio in the small backyard, basking in the late afternoon sun. In the distance, to the west, a dense fog was rolling over the hills.

"We made good timing—San Francisco is back to being itself," Patricia remarked.

"But it's always sunny in the Mission."

"As the saying goes, except on rainy days."

"Would you jump in the ocean in the fog?"

"I have, but I've seen some guys dive fully clothed with nothing warm to wear on their way out—that's just nuts. Something to say for alcohol-fueled rationale," she commented.

"Need we go there?"

"Nah, can't dwell down the old road of misery—you and I, Sir, have better things to talk about."

"Such as?"

"Remember the two of us?"

"Vaguely, but I'm sure it'll get back to me."

"Our friends got to Drake's Beach with missing information; mostly, the memory of having previously eavesdropped on that precise moment, which we assume never happened—the dream that is. What I'm saying makes sense, right?" Patricia asked.

"Please, continue."

"The information in question couldn't just be us knowing that they didn't possess it—where's the substance in that? I'm looking for something palpable."

"Everything starts out of seemingly nothing, so perhaps looking for that something isn't really the point— we have to come up with it from the knowledge it is missing, but not by foraging in the dream," John offered.

"In a nutshell, we don't know what it is, they don't have it, and the reason why we don't have it either is because is hasn't occurred yet. If you get my drift, we're going to have to pay particular attention to what's going to happen in the next couple of days," she stressed.

"Now, if memory serves, you heard my double say that a job in neuroscience would be nearly impossible for him to secure. That information is pivotal in the sense that he waited two days to let your counterpart know, but as we already explored, it isn't, in of itself, potent knowledge. My take is that my other self omitted something that was either said in that group or meant to be asked. What's missing has got to be in that conversation with my colleagues—something I must extract, since I am now aware it might hide in there," John speculated.

"That sounds like a pretty convincing argument, my dear man, I'm fairly sure you've hit the nail on the head. Now, it is up to you and your skills to pay particular attention to what is said in the thread that lies under the main topic. Think of it as two conversations: one about the reasons of your meeting, the other, about your options in regard to the two of us. Normally, what I am asking of you would pass as an unrealistic set of demands, but we are clear we're a team, so I don't need to spell what we have agreed on, right?"

"Of course."

"But I will nonetheless. There is this unspoken notion that you should be the one moving to San Francisco, while I'd just sit around doing nothing. The way I see it, and I could be wrong, is that my life here is a continuation of what I consider being my further education. It is in line with where I want to be and what I have set to achieve. I am at peace with that choice because it resonates at the highest level. Now, I am not speaking for you, John, but you have confided in me that you no longer belong to the lifestyle you accustomed yourself with in England. We have spoken about it, and you've given me all the reasons to believe that you are in a better position to come here than I am to live there. Since I don't want to go over this again, and we have committed to work as one, can you please reaffirm that it is what you want, difficult job search and all?" she implored.

"I have promised and made it clear that I would never let you down. Yes, my life in England is the one of the mask—there is nothing there that needs me, and my friends are mostly colleagues with whom I share nothing beyond work, or mundane items around a pint at the pub. My family is scattered and my son could be in Bangkok one day, and the next, in Hobart, Tasmania. So, as far as anchors are concerned, only my work at the University of Cambridge has enough fluke to keep me from drifting away. As you know, I am also at odds with the job—I have outgrown it. Does it answer your question?"

119

"Yes, thank you, John. I wasn't doubting you or myself—I just needed to firm things up once and for all. I would never demand anything of you—that's simply not me."

John knew what he had to prepare for. He made it absolute in his mind that his profession was now in the back seat of a much larger purpose. He realized what the other John had been missing: the higher drive to solidify the foundation of his relationship with an exceptionally gifted and compassionate being, one he would never encounter again in his lifetime if he were so negligent as to slacking. His choice was simple—he was moving to San Francisco no matter what. Only courage could override fear and all the other evils that hung to it, the courage to empower the self in the face of imagined adversity. He was free at last. He called the cab that would return him to the Fairmont.

7 – THE SEVENTH DAY

John awoke at six and called room service for delivery of a breakfast of coffee, fruit salad, and a bowl of muesli and yogurt. He meditated for a quick affirmation of what he had set himself to accomplish during the day. Most importantly, he couldn't lose track of the message by letting himself be distracted by the powerful habits of his profession. He was aware that one such distraction would be enough to send him back into the soft confusion of the pre-Patricia days—into the reality of the mask. There was only enough room for one John at the end of that particular Monday, and he intended it to be the one he woke up with. He had promised Patricia he would call her upon getting up, so he dialed her number and waited for her to pick-up.

"Morning, kiddo, go back to sleep—I love you!"

"Hi John, I'm up—love you too! I can't remember any dreams, so good luck with your meetings—surprise me!" she answered.

"I'm sticking to the program—forging right ahead!" he affirmed in his usual laugh.

"Great to hear!"

"How was the drumming?"

"Insanely rewarding—us girls know how to have fun—thanks for asking!"

"Pleasure—I must go, love—talk to you later!"

"Bye!"

His first meeting was at nine at UCSF on Parnassus, a place he knew well for having studied and interned there. Present were researcher Max Dawson, from

121

the university, Gerald Shumacher, head surgeon from UC Davis, and Albert Finch, senior researcher at Stanford University. John was familiar with all three from having met on numerous occasions. The main purpose of the gathering was to share notes on the latest advancements in technology and their applications in the field. It also was an opportunity to spread the methodological knowledge of their work without the scrutiny of the organizations that supported them, institutions that directly competed for the number one spot. It was a race to the finish for the three California universities, with San Francisco and Stanford barely apart by a nose.

The topic of John Leeds potentially relocating to the area didn't get breached until the end of the meeting when the four relaxed into a sense of accomplishment. Dawson's first response was, "What is Cambridge going to do without you?" But then, he added, "By the way, John, when are you planning on retiring?" Leeds had another ten years to think about it, and England wasn't the US, where early retirement was more the norm than the exception in the field.

"California is a tough market, especially at your age—we have candidates from all around the world with remarkable credentials, waiting for that one opening," Shumacher added.

"Why would you want to choose here over Cambridge, I mean, aren't you one of the most respected researchers in Europe? Plus, your books are doing well there, the last I heard," Finch said.

"There are a number of reasons for it, but mainly, there is this sense of stagnation that comes with ancient institutions that is making me feel my potential is being wasted. I envy the kind of money that is being poured into research over here. But it's definitely not a salary thing—I'm OK with what I have been making," John said.

But he realized, all too narrowly, that the mask was about to take charge. He straightened his spine and added, "Actually, I am not presenting this to you in a straightforward manner—other interests have been piquing my curiosity, some of them that run counter to our profession. I was just curious as to what my chances were in finding something in neurology. I realize now that it is nothing more than a foolish proposition. To leave what I have so painstakingly built over decades of strenuous work, for what may amount to be nothing more than the rare opportunity to lecture about what everyone already knows, is pure child fantasy. Though, I thought I could have used the change of scenery."

"Good for you, John, we need you in Cambridge—you are our strongest link to the UK," Dawson said.

"Hey, we all need to dream—I always wanted to sail around the world, but the world needs surgeons more than it needs people with too much time on their hands," Finch contributed.

"It will pass, unless there's a woman involved. If that's the case, don't do it, John!" Shumacher joked, laughing out loud.

The meeting was soon over. The four parted in the direction of their respective life's choices. There were no reasons for John to ride all the way to Palo Alto anymore—Finch didn't require it, and even if he had insisted on him going there, there would be no point to it. The mask was off.

He called Patricia to ask her out for lunch, to which she responded with unrestrained enthusiasm.

"I'm glad I opted out of my driving shift. Let's go somewhere out of the way!" she proposed

"What about that coffee shop at the end of Sloat Boulevard, what's the name?" he asked.

"Perfect—the Java Beach—I love that place!" she exclaimed.

"I'm in the Sunset, let's meet there in an hour—does it work for you?"

"I'll be there!"

— o —

Patricia and John sat at an outside table facing the zoo. The last of the Doggie Diner dog heads, across the boulevard, echoed of days long gone.

"Whoever came up with the idea of placing the zoo near the ocean, in the coldest and foggiest part of San Francisco, must have been insane," John abruptly said.

"Don't get me started on zoos!"

"Sorry, I was just thinking aloud."

"No wonder, you've been looking at the gate for two straight minutes!"

"I guess the meeting spaced me out—it was an education of sorts."

"Please, tell me how that went."

"Honestly, it was a waste. Well, I didn't see it that way at first, as I fell right back into the role—mask et al. I was John Leeds, head researcher of neuroscience at Cambridge, meeting with some US heavy lifters. It was all proper and serious—important people speaking about very important topics. I am at the top in my field back home. I am well respected, looked up to in reverence, you may even say I'm a rock star. But the second I mentioned

124

relocating to the Bay Area, it felt as if I had lowered my credibility in their eyes—I became the outsider, something they didn't want to touch. If I had never met you, I would have taken it as a welcome challenge, selling myself with unrestrained confidence, pairing my experience to substantial contribution in the field of research with the aim of swaying votes, going the length to persuade them that they wouldn't be able to live without me—that science couldn't progress without my contribution. I almost went there—the mask almost took on the fight. But I refrained. I could no longer go on with the game. I just told them it was just a silly idea and so to forget about it. Somehow, I wonder if they took it as me losing my drive."

"You make it sound like a defeat. Are you having second thoughts?"

"It's not what I mean. I am utterly tired of it—I didn't realize to what extent until today. I will apply for early retirement at Cambridge—if they let me—otherwise, I will simply let the job go. It'll disappoint some colleagues, but I'm beyond caring."

"How are you going to fare financially?"

"I don't know—I shall think of something. I have a few assets. I can let the house to interns, sell a few odd things. I feel both free and vacuous right now, so it's best that I don't think too logically. I fear the other John let the mask take over. It's a battle he cannot win—I saw it in the metaphorical tea leaves."

"Are you saying that the two we eavesdropped on in the dream are doomed?"

"I believe they are in some way. Perhaps they will still give it a try, but if the mask doesn't fall, it won't last, because your double won't let it happen."

"You make it sound like your counterpart won't keep his end of the bargain. Don't you think the two of them are equally responsible for the outcome?"

"My counterpart thinks he is keeping his end of the bargain, but I know him—I know the mask. On the other hand, I have to assume they both work from a common script," John concurred.

"So, you threw the mask away?"

"The mask is no more, Patricia, but it put on a good fight."

"I feel your pain; I know it's not easy, John."

"As I said, I feel liberated, so the pain is just part of the healing. I'm blessed to have your understanding."

"Well, since we're a team, I have to also make concessions at my end. For one thing, I'm done with cab-driving. I was going to work today, but last night, after drumming, I decided that I didn't have to sell myself short any longer. Let's face it—it's a shit sandwich, and all the romanticizing around it is overrated BS. The idea that a cabdriver is some kind of bohème is an illusion entertained by those who don't have the courage to call themselves cabdrivers. They are the writers who have been working on their first book for the last twenty years, the musicians with claims of great chops, but who never have anything to show for; the painters whose work gets ignored in wi-fi joints... I have six books, I'm in a rocking drum group, I paint from the heart and my work is well received—I don't belong in a cab, John, and that's a scary thought—time for Patricia's mask to fall too!"

"You have my vote of confidence—I'm sure you will do very well. I also have means beyond the lab. I'm a published writer—I don't need to be tied to a place to keep on writing. I've got a few new ideas that will nicely complement my previous work, and which may please the holistic crowd. That came out of left field at our meeting today, I almost didn't heed its mention."

"That sounds like a great pointer—John Leeds the writer—how perfect! Could it be the item the other you missed to capitalize on?"

"It definitely could. I always thought the writing was integral to my work at Cambridge, but actually, it doesn't have to—I had missed on the distinction."

"I'm not saying it settles it, but it suggests a valid direction. It may not be much, but as you said, big things come out of seemingly nothing," she returned, excited.

Their conversation was momentarily interrupted by a chain of events that involved a Toyota Prius pulling behind a black and heavily modded diesel Dodge Ram truck at a red light. The suspect vehicle was vibrating from the massive bass thump coming from its high-wattage sound system. Inside, a group of four men in their twenties appeared to display unusual excitement, one of them seen behind the tinted glass, drinking from a bottle of Jack Daniels. Just as the light turned green, the roar of the engine was followed by a thick black cloud, enveloping the Prius and bringing doom down on the boulevard, all the way to the beach, while shouts of victory coupled to horrific insults aimed at liberals, were heard amid the mayhem. In contrast, the Toyota sat until the soot settled around it, and then proceeded, noiseless and smokeless.

"Any black residue floating in you coffee, dear?" John humored.

"I kinda knew what those fuckers were up to, so I memorized their plate number before they took off. Is rolling coal the thing in England too?"

"It would be if they could afford the gas oil for these sorts of vehicles. Luckily, the closest we come to this nasty trend is an old four-banger with bad injectors. These people seemed rather agitated—what was their point exactly, proving that a ruined planet is a better place to live on than a green one?"

"Pretty much—this shit isn't even legal in California, but the cops aren't doing a lot about it."

"No need to let it spoil the day—clueless maniacs have roamed the Earth since humans grew legs."

"I wish they'd gone the way of the dinosaurs," she said, resigned.

"It must have been an administrative error. The maniacs were the ones scheduled for extinction, but you know how that goes..." he said, trying to light things up.

"Sorry, John, I'm still shaken. I'm having a hard time enjoying the humor in it."

"Fancy a cookie? I'm getting one and a refill."

"I'll split one."

"Alright—any coffee?"

While John was busy at the counter, Patricia cogitated on her mood swing. Yes, it was shocking to witness firsthand a bunch of rednecks coming unstitched on whatever drugs and booze they were on, on a Monday afternoon, but she had to lighten up. No need to paint the world grey when the sun shone in her heart. There was a lot more good than bad in the universe, otherwise there would be nothing left of it, she mused. It was simple enough logic, something the soul could understand. She relaxed, taking in the realization she was officially in a relationship—with a man, of all things. Most of the girls in the group had been supportive. To her surprise, one of the lesbians turned to her and said, "I might not like men, but I'd have a hard time turning down a prince—good luck, darling!"

John returned with the fares.

"I see, you bought two cookies?"

"You didn't say you wanted to split equally."

"Did I have to? That's the point of sharing."

"Fear not, the second one is for sharing later."

"You're a gentleman."

"I try to be—thanks. I thought a walk would be nice, how is Lake Merced, I've never been there?"

"It's mostly a golf course. When at the beach, I recommend sticking to the beach. There are some decent dune trails at Fort Funston, south of here, if you want some diversity."

"Splendid!"

— o —

It was on one of the trails that John posed a question from left field that seemed to dangerously flirt with contradiction.

"How can we be sure the dream has any bearing on reality and that we're not simply creating an elaborate scenario out of nothing, or simply for the sake of enforcing our theory about *the shifts*?"

"I hope you're just asking for the sake of asking, and not being swayed by doubt, John."

"I think it's worth considering if we're not meant to leave any stones unturned."

"The way I see it, you just moved one that had already been turned. Then, what was the point of finding ourselves awake in the dream—is the gist of that realization escaping you?" she asked, befuddled.

129

"Using your terminology, that stone wasn't as much turned as it was jarred. Finding ourselves aware in a reality that somewhat resembles our own, doesn't make that reality genuine. We could just as easily have created it as a background to analyze possibilities."

"You're saying that our counterparts and the drive on Shoreline Highway was possibly a construct—then for what purpose?"

"You said it yourself, and we both agreed that those two were only representations of ourselves in a closely matched setup further in time—but were they really us?" he posed.

"As part of exploring all possibilities, I am willing to play the game, so here we go! Even if we end up not going to Drake's Beach on Wednesday, it doesn't change a thing. The fork in the road happened either at the moment we found ourselves in the dream, or earlier, so by then, our respective realities will have had plenty of time to substantially veer from each other. Furthermore, in the case the other two don't exist and the trip to the beach never happened, we still woke up with questions that determined a course to be followed. We pretty much knew then that if we were to doubt our relationship, it would not survive. So, to me, real or not, what came out of it is the only thing that matters. Doubt is central to defeating what we have built in our short time together and now would be the perfect moment to introduce it as an actor, to wrap up the perfect Shakespearian tragedy. Is it where we're at, John, at a time of unraveling of dreams and hopes? Aren't you aware that you walking out now would qualify as a major low in my life? What is it that is gnawing at your thinking process, John, especially right after claiming the mask was off for good?"

"Maybe that fear/trust stone hasn't been fully turned. Perhaps the magnitude of the necessary changes outweighs the promise."

"Oh, John, is that what you believe...?"

"Is it not worth considering, not as doubt, but rather, as an honest attempt at erasing doubt?"

"It sure sounds like you're not exactly trying to not instill doubt to the process. So, to get to the fucking point, was the meeting that bad?" a teary Patricia asked.

"It could be that the meeting stirred a renewed appreciation for my past achievements in the light of losing my reputation, but I'm at peace with that—those fears are mine to bear, and I'm sure I can handle them. No, I trust you and the choice we have made. As I said, I would never betray you, but the dream has been nagging at me. Even though I agree that what emanated from it is more important than the content, I am still interested in understanding the mechanics of it. We have ascertained that, in the dream, we observed other versions of ourselves on our way to Drake's Beach, but when we go there on Wednesday, it will be us. What stops me from imagining that we didn't build on that vision?"

"But why a construct, John, what difference does it make? In a sense, you're aiming at invalidating that vision. Where is the line that defines the real from the illusion—you tell me! Aren't you basically turning our experience into an object of science? It won't allow you, John, because the rational mind has no place in it. It is the world of intuition, a place to observe from the standpoint of neutrality, and to embrace with blessed naiveté. Don't do it, John, don't leave me alone as you walk away from faith, or you are going to make me believe the mask is back, claiming a space it has no right

131

to own. You said it yourself, I won't let you do it—and you were right."

"Forgive me—I needed to hear you say it. My department of intuition is new in the business," John finally capitulated, knowing that something in him had crossed the line.

"At least, give us the chance to reach Wednesday before coming up with theories and counter-theories. We agreed we were taking a step into the unknown, so let's not anticipate what it might be until we see it—can we do that, John?" Patricia practically begged.

"I see where I might have lost my footing, Patricia—something to do with being in charge of my environment. In reality, I don't fathom I have ever been in control of it, just the material side of it, but even that was an illusion—the whole bloody thing was. And now that I have slowly been coming to grips with the fact, latent fears are crawling through the cracks with more untruths. For Christ's sake, will it ever end?!"

"Change is a difficult thing, even when it comes to leaving abuse. So, believe me when I say I understand."

"It has been said that some of us, in the field, have developed a god complex. Perhaps all the years of being at the top of the think-tank have imprinted that stigma onto my person. In that case, the mask may be made of layers."

"You're just freaking out, John, if you don't mind me saying. Honestly, I kind of was hoping it wouldn't happen, but it doesn't surprise me—we're only human—even on our best behavior we manage to err. I would take you to a bar if I knew it could help, but I'm afraid it would take you over the edge, rather."

"I'm not depressed—I have no reason to be. It's mostly intellectually-based panic. Something in me is trying to coerce me back into thinking logically, deeming that leaving everything behind is the most irrational move I could ever make. I'm sure that many in my entourage will agree—you just can't ignore the sheer magnitude of peer pressure. I didn't anticipate I had so many buried elements within me. I guess that as long as I gave them a comfortable place to exist, they didn't have to make noise. Now that they are being evicted, I'm never going to hear the end of it, am I?" John said, trying to regain his sense of humor.

"No doubt you'll have to hear from the inner peanut gallery—think of it as entertainment," she joked, unsure of whether or not it was the right thing to do.

"Thanks for the vote of confidence, my friend."

Patricia hadn't expected John to come back from his meeting so bent out of shape. She felt terrible since he was the one going through the big change, while all that was required of her was to wait for him to get over it. How would she fare if she had to abandon all she had, to start a new life in Britain? There was only one San Francisco, a beautiful city bursting with energy, at the cutting edge of most things—how would Cambridge fare against that? She didn't remember hearing much about the town, apart from its famous campus. Maybe it was a wild place too, for which she might develop a taste. But she couldn't feel it—there was only a void unlikely to be filled by the love of another. John had confessed he was left with few options in his community, besides surrendering to quaint commonality and stagnation. So, in spite of the resistance that had abruptly mounted, it was clear the success of their relationship hinged on his ability to stick to his word and overcome whatever was putting up a fight. She wanted it to be a different kind of battle for John, not one that had festered from within to reclaim what was due, but rather, a last ditch effort by the mask not to be taken into the chasm of forgetfulness, a desperate reflex in the face of an inevitable death.

"I can almost hear your thoughts—are you contemplating what it would be if our roles were reversed?" John asked.

"Your department of intuition is back on track. Yes, actually, I was thinking about how miserable life would be away from all the things I love. It might sound heartless, but I didn't meet you because some barking pheromones advertised Patricia was desperate to live in the UK and you took the call—I believe it is you who called for someone to rescue you from your life in Britain. I didn't know it then, but it also happened I was on the lookout for a soul to help me refocus on my true self—so it's a balanced act. I keep on feeling guilty about the San Francisco/Cambridge thing, but I shouldn't—the pieces are set. Rather, it all hinges on where we wish to belong at the heart level and the essence of choice; if you know what I'm trying to get at," she replied.

"I think I do, but we know guilt is utterly useless. I have chosen, so there is nothing else to talk about. I shall make all the necessary arrangements and keep you informed along the way. You are of course aware that we must marry in order for me to reside in the US. I don't expect a lavish affair—a reverend, a witness, and a couple of inexpensive rings will do, but it's up to you what you want to do with it. I'm not going to take long with my things, so there won't be the interminable months of seeing through logistics and other items of posturing around unexpected delays. I'm saying two months top. It's the last call—are you ready for the journey?"

"That was a quick turnaround, John. I know faith when I feel it, so I appreciate your integrity. It's bound to be a wild ride, but I wouldn't expect otherwise."

"I just had to go over it in my head—nothing so fundamental as to doubting the self. I wanted to be honest with what I was going through—I think I owed that to you. I know the timing was odd, or maybe it was just in the way I presented it. I hope it settles things. But you didn't respond about the marriage..."

"Of course, I'm going to marry you, John! That would be wicked of me to bring you here and then say no. But I insist you ask properly—a wild thing is still allowed to be old-fashioned when it matters," she said, relieved they had safely made it past the hurdle.

"Then allow me to pick the time and space—give me time to think about it."

"As long as you do your best to make it look like a surprise—but don't linger, sweet man."

— o —

Save for the early days, John's heart had never been too far from San Francisco. Not only had he studied there, but for the many years that followed, he had attended its yearly medical and pharmaceutical summits, partaken in innumerable conferences, as well as lectured on the results of his research. He soon developed a taste for the city, using every opportunity offered to him to explore its hidden resources, its arts, its history, and the lesser traveled paths of its everyday workings – the ways that were often taken for granted by its denizens. In the end, he knew as much as there was to know about it from the standpoint of the average San Franciscan. His

135

knowledge of the city was the proxy of his resident status, a state that, over the years, had found its way into his psyche, practically unnoticed. He also had visited on many occasions with his wife Jane – using his vacation time as a pretext to follow his heart. Jane didn't mind, she too enjoyed the Bay Area, but she preferred New York for its theaters and stores – she loved shopping. Mostly, she savored hearing herself name the two cities during social gatherings back home. It was, "When John and I were in San Francisco, this," and, "When John and I were in New York, that." It used to amuse him, but towards the later years of their relationship, it began to exasperate him. On their final trips together, he left her in New York, while he continued on to San Francisco. She had made many friends on the East Coast, no longer caring about what he had to say or did. Jane was the English socialite par excellence, what the Americans unflatteringly referred to as a phony. She was a woman of airs and little substance, using manners to disguise a lack of. Even though John knew what he had married into, marriage was only one of the things you had to check off in life – he had a wife, and that was all society expected of him. After a while, love and sex became mere afterthoughts. Jane was too much in her head to enjoy sex anyway, and John was too busy with his work to care whether she did or not. Sex was scantly more than a mechanical thing between two people who had fallen out of low elevation love. "Barely a chair's height," he had once humored.

John wasn't always faithful to the relationship, and he later discovered Jane hadn't been either. He had a difficult time imagining how someone could have been enamored of her, but he had to concede to the vivid possibility he and Jane had never been made for each other. The pointed irony was felt like a dagger in his pride – he too had been a fake. The thought had resurfaced with the understanding that there was no redemption in not being authentic. Patricia had long known about it, and so had he. But while she applied the maxim of authenticity to her life by turning down the bullshit, as she called it, he had seen it as a concept without virtue in a world full of insincerity. For all intents and purposes, apathy justified the mask. But much water had passed under the bridge that connected the shores of denial to those of reason, and ample meditation was spent on the self during the years that followed the divorce. His son, James, had also seen that he let go of the old ways, while growing a modicum of awareness in the process. Much was owed to him in that respect, in spite of the countless battles. Or perhaps, it was the battles that did the trick, by weakening the hubris of stubborn blindness.

As part of the education, his profession started to see the soil come loose around its base. The world was not painted in the black and white of rigid science, and it was clear that with every new discovery, the credibility of rhetoric was rapidly losing its sheen. There were unquestionable advancements, but they often seemed stifled by the lack of hindsight – by the systematic refusal to acknowledge the accidents often directly responsible for them, or by not taking into account the parallel realities from which those very achievements sprang.

Meeting Patricia was a clear indicator of what he had attained through his years of self-exploration. She, as part of the sequence that developed from the time they met at the airport, represented the apogee of a primal phase, the completion of a stage ahead of another. *Shift number three* was the test, the final exam before the beginning of the journey to consciousness' higher grounds. But the latest lapse into doubt wasn't just about the relationship, it was about the fundamental makeup of his being – he was doubting what went against the established logical, the male was pushing the female out of bounds with the aim of capitalizing on the penalty, and he was ashamed of what had just happened. In a way, he had tried to diminish himself in Patricia's eyes, unconsciously matching the figure he had projected before his colleagues when he informed them of his desire to leave Cambridge. But it was all in his head. It was certain they protected their turf, but it was unlikely they had perceived a weakness – they were too rational to deduct from intuition. That was forbidden territory, a danger zone better left alone. He needed to atone for having slipped, but gracefully. Silence was far better than uttering the wrong excuse. Anything but honesty would send him reeling into self-deprecation. The mere thought nauseated him. What was happening to him? It was a seismic event, a jarring of identity faults, a shifting of emotional tectonic plates. But what better time for it to happen than now, right when it mattered. Maybe something was finally letting go because of the relative safety of the moment, in the presence of someone who understood about inner struggles. He came to recognize there was nowhere to go but surrender and admit to his humanity. The thought comforted him.

— o —

"Why don't you grab your things from the hotel and come stay with me for the remainder of your visit? I believe it's time you get out of that sterile, fake floral-smelling room," Patricia offered, as they walked back towards the zoo and Sloat Boulevard.

"Thank you, I think I will, Patricia. I could use your soothing presence—I feel a bit fragile."

"To own one's moment of weakness is to show one's strength," she praised.

"Thank you, Patricia."

"Let's hop on the L-Taraval—it'll take us down Market, then we can grab a cab from the hotel to my place, if that's OK with you?"

"Perfect, I love street cars. We call them trams in Britain. Too bad London pulled them out of service in 1952, although new lines opened in 2000."

"Why were they taken out?"

"They were claimed to be expensive to build and maintain. The new equipment is a lot lighter and less costly, but the future of the new lines is constantly compromised by politics—the much advertised Oxford Street tram, due to open this year, succumbed to the axe."

"I think they make a city friendlier, but we are blessed here with the vintage cars of the Market Street line. I believe the oddest-looking ones, which resemble boats more than they do cars, come from the North of England—Blackpool, I was told."

"Yes, I've seen one of them. Blackpool is a resort town, so they were built on an amusement park theme, as much for looks as function. They were fair weather contraptions that fit poorly in a not-so-fair-weather town."

"They're a happy pair here—well loved," Patricia said, snuggling against John in the seat of their own departing car.

That evening, after a light vegan dinner of beets, tempeh, and greens, they lit candles and listened to music from South America. They went to bed early, letting the voices of Amazonian pan flutes take them into sleep.

— o —

John Leeds heard an unfamiliar noise. Aided by the faint glow of the city lights filtered by the curtains, he got up and made his way across the room to the door. He looked into the long hall lit by rows of etched-glass sconces. All he saw was the back of the room service employee pushing his cart. He must have been dreaming, he thought, and just then, he remembered what the dream had been about—a long walk on the beach with a woman he didn't know. Yet, there was the kind of intimacy between them that made him wish he was back with her. He returned to the bed, in hopes of catching the tail of it. But instead, he lay there, unable to sleep, trying to latch onto the wondrous feeling of being around that magical being. Who was she? Where did his love for this mysterious stranger come from? She seemed so perfect, so full of wisdom and goodness, but she was a dream creature, elusive and soon to be forgotten. His stay in San Francisco had been uneventful—same faces, same new gadgets, same as always. Two more days before he would be back in Cambridge, where he was scheduled to lecture on the latest in robotics for the operating room. Finally, he went back to sleep. By the time he got up, the woman of the dream was long gone.

— o —

In another place, John woke up to the sound of his pounding heart. His chest actually hurt. He eased his body into a more peaceful rhythm, reminding himself everything was alright. The little he remembered of the dream was obscured by a sense of immense disorientation and loss. Within it, there had been another dream, and yet others beyond it. Each of them came with a longing to return to the previous one—to finish what was started. But with every awakening, he felt dragged deeper into the layers, while the distance between him and Patricia widened out of reach and hope. When he finally calmed himself down enough to claim a semblance of sanity, he was alone in his hotel room, surrendering to the notion something had gone awfully wrong. Then he heard a distant voice.

"It's alright, John, it's only a nightmare—you're safe here with me."

He opened his eyes. Patricia had switched on the light. He looked at her as she smiled the smile of someone who deeply cared. He was home at last. He pressed his body against hers. The room returned to darkness. All was well in the world.

8 – THE EIGHTH DAY

The early morning sun shone from across the lemon tree outside, past the wooden slats of the window shades, and through the rich colored patterns of Patricia's hand-painted curtains, projecting dancing figures in all areas of the bedroom. She tried to remember her dreams, but aside from seeming odd, they didn't offer anything of significance. John was still sleeping. She wasn't too concerned about what had happened last night, but she was sorry to see him go through a hard time. Obviously, his later choices had broken the vacuum of sealed spaces, releasing a few screaming banshees in the process. She got up, making sure to not stir him out of his needed rest, and shut the door behind her. The kitchen window faced the house next door where she could see a woman in the nude going about her business of preparing for the day. The two were in the habit of waving at each other from across the space, like silent accomplices in the act of letting it all out. Patricia wished the whole world could be as free as they were in that moment bereft of bullshit. She made coffee before using the bathroom to brush her teeth and comb her hair. She would take a shower later, so as to not lock John out of the room when he got up. She spread the Chronicle on the kitchen table, loosely checking for news that didn't involve the president. She had promised to ignore the man, regardless of the headline bait. He didn't deserve the attention—no-one that imbecilic did. The country was addicted to shining a light on mediocrity and decadence, as if to put a disclaimer on its own. Russians or not, he was who the citizenry, mostly on account of epic booth desertion, had elected as their official representative to the rest of the world. "So, live with it, country, and clean up your own mess instead of whining!" she once exclaimed. She checked the movie section—she still had to see *The Shape of Water*. In spite of the Oscar, some reviewers had maligned it by pitting it against another Del Toro masterpiece, to the effect that it was deemed too unrealistic, and that its physics were faulty. "Perhaps someone needed to be reminded of the meaning of the word *fantasy*. Another demonstration of the irrationality of human rationale," she thought.

She heard stirring in the bedroom. By the time John came out, she had put some clothes on and was getting ingredients out of the fridge for breakfast.

"Good morning, sir!"

"How do, kiddo!" he answered, half asleep.

They hugged and kissed.

"Got to use the commodities before I can make myself available," he humored.

"When I visited New York City, I stayed with friends on the Upper East Side who had the bathtub in the kitchen. I wonder how it would be to prepare breakfast while your husband's dick is kinda floating to the surface," she punned.

"I'll take that thought with me to the loo!"

"So, what was that all about, John?" she asked, as he later joined in the kitchen.

"I don't recall ever finding myself unable to get out of the dream state—it was awful."

"Any leads as to why?"

"I could always speculate, since it was essentially a spiral into losing you, as I was taken farther and farther into the strata, while you seem to clench to something or be held by some form of tether. The most frightening thing was that it felt like more than one of me was dreaming. I'm not even sure I'm not still in it—it was that disorientating," he tried to explain.

"I am of the belief that when you enter the deep layers of the self, you end up merging with probable realities, and becoming entangled with the experiences of selves on dissimilar courses, each with their own opening on a reality that shares the same background—the world may give the appearance of normalcy, but the locations and times may be quite disparate, like mole holes on a golf course, say."

"Potent metaphor, Patricia! So, using that train of thought, below the surface is this maze of tunnels that not only travel sideways, but up and down as well, right?"

"In our version of time and space, yes. Of course, it would also include all the past and future mounds and tunnels, as well as the mole's ability to exist in all locations simultaneously."

"Heady indeed—it felt as if I were dragged down deeper, while striving to reach the surface, with every pull, losing you more," he described.

"It sounds like you've really pissed someone off in those depths of yours."

"The crux of it, Patricia, is that I couldn't prevent losing you, until I finally reached the bottom and you could no longer be seen. At that point, it felt like I was eavesdropping on someone dreaming of a you they had never met, all because I was close enough for him to access my memory. By then, I strongly believed I had become irreversibly mad."

"Some would pay a lot of money to be able to do what you did. It reminds me of Christopher Nolan's

Inception—I'm sure you've either seen or heard of the movie. Of course, your experience is no Hollywood fantastic sci-fi story—it's the real thing, the descent into the cavework of the self. It's a world where information is shared, never stolen—and even if that information appears locked in dark rooms at the end of dusty hallways, the keys are in the hands of all of your selves," she explained.

"By the sound of it, I imagine you've been there before."

"Oh, I have, but only through the intuitive channels, trying my very best to not take my fears along with me. I have strived to stay lucid in the dream state, though I admit that the results have been scant, since they have a lot to do with memory and how the experience translates at the waking level. Obviously, the physics are quite dissimilar. But during meditation, all it takes is for me to be willing to inspect the nature of beliefs and access the ones that have become invisible, while still playing an enormous part in my daily life. Those are the prized items. But they can fight back, and depending on the playfield, the methodology can be quite creative, swinging from a game of smoke and mirrors, to a downright attack on the body," she explained.

"Or bloody nightmares."

"That would be when a whole bunch of them go on the charge—just kidding!"

"I like your keen interpretation of your travels— very visual. It helps me better understand the mechanics of my own explorations—though, I would prefer if I had a say in the timing."

"Then it's all the better reason to try to locate that clock and its accompanying compass."

"Should you have a metaphor for every occasion?"

"Metaphors explain in layers what the intellectual deductive process loses in tedious linearity. Or is that too metaphorical for you, sir?"

"I only meant to be inquisitorially playful, Ms."

"And I, metaphorically so. You want eggs or is it too un-vegan?" she countered with a wink.

"You have a way of volleying a response into a goal—I love your style, girl. But yes, eggs would be fine—want a hand with them?"

"I'm alright lifting them out of the carton, but I could need your help hauling the shells away—then you can mince chives," she said, barely containing a straight face.

"Thanks for that, Patricia, I am now certain I just found my true reality again," he humored back.

"Anything else you wish to talk about, concerning your nightmare?" she asked, back to being serious.

"I remember waking up in my hotel room when I should have been here, next to you—that was particularly disturbing."

"Do you think that could have been the you of the Shoreline Highway to Drake's Beach? What if, in that reality, I didn't offer for you to move in with me?"

"Yes, it makes so much sense—that gives me chills."

"That would be the kind of drift I was talking about yesterday—them and us are veering away from each other. Do we still care about going to Point Reyes tomorrow?"

"Didn't you say you wanted to badly? I personally think we should go as planned. I don't know why, Patricia, but I sense there is something there."

146

"I just don't want to gc for the sake of discovering a link between the two realities. You remember my ulterior motive, don't you, John?"

"I do—I certainly don't want to miss that!"

"Yeah, it's just perfect—a conclusion with roots in its beginning—my kind of ritual!"

"The full initiation of *shift number three* as a gateway into the sublime unknown!" he rejoiced.

— o —

Patricia and John took their coffee mugs to the private backyard. No-one lived upstairs, while the vegetation sheltered them from the buildings next door.

"It's my sunbathing area. Right there, in that corner of the grass, nobody can see me when I'm in the nude—it's the miracle spot. I think it can fit two. If you're into it when the light reaches it in the mid-afternoon, you and I can roast a bit—I'll massage you with a special oil infused with St. John's wort that I harvested on my last camping trip."

"There must be a hidden apothecary in you as well. I'll be delighted to return the favor, if you're into it, that is," he played. "By the way, why is the upstairs vacant?"

"I use it as my art studio and guest area—I own the building."

"Impressive—how were you able to afford it on your cabdriver's income?"

"I inherited it from a dear friend who passed. All I had to do was take over the last five years of the mortgage payments—a gift from the universe. I could make a bundle renting half of it, but I like having a big place. There's also the basement, which I turned into a

147

soundproofed studio for the drumming, as well as a large attic space under the mansard roof that could potentially be renovated into a rental—for now, it's used as storage."

"Wow, you're full of surprises, Ms. Reyes. Now I'm convinced Cambridge was never an option for you."

"Glad you see it that way. It will make matters a lot smoother when the time comes for you to move in. I don't expect you'll wish to keep separate quarters."

"I haven't thought thus far, but now that you tell me, I don't see the point of hunting for a larger place together. I mean, even the one apartment is plenty sufficient for the two of us, although, I care very much about the sanctity of your space."

"Thank you, John, but I'm OK with it and it's very likely that it'll stay that way. As you say, there's plenty of room for two—unless of course, we start disliking each other," she teased.

"As long as I can have a room as my office/private space, I'm certain to be very pleased with the arrangement. Of course, as I said, I will have some capital—so, no worries in that department."

"It's a large three bedroom apartment, John—no doubt you'll find comfort in one of the spare rooms. I'll move the extra junk to the attic. I'll take you around as soon as we're done with our coffees."

"Dropping the mask doesn't necessarily mean that I'm abandoning my work—I definitely am ready to take it in a different direction though. What I'm saying is that it would be nice if I had fast internet," he enquired.

"Not to worry, John, the house's cabled. The basement studio is wired for Skype sessions—we invite players from around the world and record them in protools. I doubt you'll need that kind of speed, but if you do, it's right here."

"Astonishing—I can't wait for it to happen!"

"That's the John I love—let me show you around the place then!"

— o —

Except for a shopping trip in anticipation of the next day's picnic at Drake's Beach, and a one hour walk around the Mission, Patricia and John stayed home, making plans for the future. It was a welcome distraction to the more existential forays of the past few days, as they instead immersed themselves in the mild logistics of time, space, and finances. As it turned out, Patricia also owned a car she rarely used. The mid-aught Nissan Altima was garaged a block away, in a space she rented from a friend. John wondered why she hadn't made mention of it. Surely, they could have used of it in lieu of calling cabs and riding buses clear across town.

"It's just a reflex from my work as a driver. I don't want to chauffeur anyone, including myself, during my spare time. I only use the car for long trips or emergencies," she explained. "But I see no reason in not taking it to Point Reyes tomorrow. Actually, it would be fitting of *the shift*—a symbolic move in the right direction, if you see where I'm going. The one thing I'm asking of you is that you'll be in charge of the driving— do we have a deal?"

"OK Ms, I'll be your chauffeur. You can always enthrall me with stories, and compliment me on my right lane driving skills."

"Sounds like an agreeable arrangement."

"I'm inclined to think that you had planned on using it all along. I mean, you could just as easily have not mentioned you owned a car until a later time."

"Your read me well. Until today, I considered quite a few things as belonging to my private world. But you've made it clear, in the light of your revelations about your fears and your general willingness to put it all on the table, that I had no valid grounds to keep things away from you. I trust we're beyond trying to guard our personal lives—at least, that's where I'm at if you're not."

"I appreciate greatly—I'm an open book, Patricia. Both of us know too well that there is no place to hide— never is, never has been. Lies don't hide the truth—they highlight it in a shameful way. Believe me, I learned the hard way," he confessed.

"We all have lied. I still catch myself doing it in small ways—mostly to protect something that might not need protection."

"It's incredible what hiding and lying have in common—again, fear based items."

"Once, I came across interesting data regarding fear and paranoia, claiming there were two kinds: natural and manufactured. The first one was instinctual—a response to real danger, such as an attack, or a catastrophic situation, like an earthquake, say; the other pertained to imagined threats, such as those induced by the pharmaceutical industry in its calculated claims that the body and the natural environment are the enemy; assumptions of danger around certain groups of people, generally fueled by xenophobia, racism, even sexism—in a nutshell, fears attached to the disempowerment of the self via bogus beliefs."

"One of the hot topics of my next book!"

"That should sit well with your colleagues—or is it ex-colleagues?" she teased.

"About to become exes—but my field is in fixing damaged people, not forcing tablets onto them. It makes for a fundamental difference in my view."

"Are you telling me that neurosurgeons rely more on the body's ability to heal itself than, say, your regular MD?"

"They do, but that would be truer if they actually believed it, meaning, they still miss on who's the better healer. That ties into the God complex, but it doesn't take away from their tremendous skills and unmitigated commitment. They are still heroes, regardless."

"You'd better make sure you let them know—you can only successfully ruffle feathers with respect."

"Ah, the miracle of metaphors! I assume said respect comes with a proper soft-grip handle."

"The one designed for you, Johnny-boy, comes with extra hard bristles and a handle for two-hand use: the Acme model 900 industrial ruffler, with tough-love attachment," she volleyed.

"Ouch! Kill me with humor, darling Patricia."

"You will eventually learn not to walk into it, darling John," she said with a straight face, before bursting into laughter.

"Is *ruffler* even a word?" he asked.

"Ask Shakespeare, he'll tell ya!"

"I see I can't win at this, but you certainly know how to cheer me up," he conceded.

"Don't be shy—you had me in stitches not so long ago. Providing that humor isn't used to hide true feelings, I see it as being the sign of a healthy personality. No doubt we feed off each other—I quite enjoy it."

"In that case, walking into it might not be so bad."

"You're always welcome to my web," she closed.

— o —

The oiling and tanning session ended in two intertwined bodies rolling in the grass, perhaps a little off the safe zone. But there was trust that no obvious indecency was exposed and reported. As to the ones fortunate enough to have, from the distance of their dwellings, and with the aid of binoculars, witnessed the sudden appearance of a sexually suggestive act in their field of vision, Patricia and John were glad these souls had something to break the boredom of their lonely afternoon with.

"What's the penalty for lewdness in this town?" John asked.

"Depends on what you mean by it, but it's hard to shock this city. For example, one time, at a red light, a naked dude jumped on the hood of my cab while on my way to bringing an elderly Midwest couple, from the airport to their hotel. The guy crouched on all fours, like a wild beast looking fiercely at us from across the windshield with his dick hanging. It was noon, the passengers were horrified, but I had to make light of it—so I said, 'Welcome to San Francisco!'"

"So, no penalty for being on peyote, blocking traffic in the nude, while impersonating a leopard?"

"You can't even make the news with that kind of shit, John. So if your Union Jack stands proud in my backyard, Britain will unfortunately never hear of it."

"By Jove, Patricia, you are going to kill me!" he exclaimed, unable to contain laughter.

"Back in the early eighties, the city had to close the Union Square men's room, because gay studs used to openly fuck each other in there, while businessmen and various other voyeurs perversely watched. Needless to say, that was a double-edged sword for the tourist business, sending some reeling, while the leather-clad hordes from Berlin and London packed our hotels," she added.

"Is that a fact?"

"The tourist metaphor is one for the law of averages—it's only partially true. But the bit about the bathrooms is verifiable," Patricia avowed.

"I can hardly imagine the odd bit of needing to go badly, only to find all the stalls occupied by randy, male actors engaging in sodomy. It is definitely one for the memory book," he humored.

"Would you be shocked if it happened to you, John?"

"Very unlikely—if anything, I am fairly sure I would find it somewhat surreal in an artistic sense."

"That's an interesting response—can you explain the artistic reference?"

"Jaundice lights, smell of urine, a row of repeated motifs and motions, and a line of immobile watchers in an interplay of release and repression borne of socio-religious oppression—envision the painting, Patricia."

"There's something in that creative mind of yours that speaks of decadence as seen at some of the most risqué exhibits of European art houses, or across the work of the likes of Fernando Arrabal—sort of heavy on deviant sexual symbolism."

"I can always find hidden beauty in the shadow of humanity. I have seen my share of horror—you can either try to shield yourself from it or embrace it. For every

153

survivor of trauma, there is the miracle of healing—a quivering strand of light that weaves in and out of shattered bone and ghastly wounds. Perhaps I'm one of the few to see it, but the work of unlikely repair is pure art to me. Life is the mother of all art!"

"Fair enough my good man—the words of a true artist. But how does public lewdness tie to injury?"

"Social trauma leads to stigmatic behavior, which I perceive as a form of injury that isn't so different from that of the body. I am not speaking for homosexuality, which has nothing to do with it, but of the deep wounds afflicted by repression from historical oppression. I see the bathroom scene as such a wound,"

Now, I am curious about your books—are you sure they only delve in science?"

"Should you dare venture into the maze, my darling, you can be the judge," he replied—amused.

"So, if I'm correct, you liken the healing process to art, and to some extent, creation?"

"It's not a law—just a personal interpretation of the nature of existence. When I say life is art, I mean it from the deep understanding that art is creation in the making. On the other hand, when that process ends into the staticity of the final work, art continues along a new creative path, as it falls under the stewardship of the masses, who, via bundled evaluation and unique construals, keep it alive," John explained.

"In other words, you are saying art can never be static, not even a painting."

"A concealed painting from the public by the artist is a prisoner. It isn't dead—simply dormant, or at a stage of unrealized potential. It becomes a reflection of that artist's deep insecurities, or over-bloated sense of proprietorship. It never truly rises from irrelevance as art. Oppositely, a painting destroyed after it has been released from the hands of the artist and displayed for viewing, can remain alive indefinitely."

"I'm not always sure of your choice of words, but I fully agree that art is never static as long as it does the rounds. The public is as much the artist as the creator is, or vice versa," she concurred.

"My mind is a cauldron above an ardent fire, Patricia – hard to keep thoughts from boiling over."

"From the man who remarks on my use of metaphors." she pointed with mild sarcasm.

"I love fitting metaphors, but I so immensely enjoy playing with you and seeing myself destroyed by your quick wits, that I can't help asking for more."

"You're total game, John—no need to ever worry about boredom between us."

"That is as secure an asset as you'll ever get—guaranteed to yield!"

"OK, John, we've gone from sex to art via the side lanes, but I will not be taken into the nefarious reality of business—time to put on some clothes and get the car ready for tomorrow!"

"I'm prepared to poke under the old bonnet when you are, mi amor."

"Just checking the oil and filling-up on Valencia—we're not rebuilding the carb, dearest John."

"It sounds like you've done motor work before."

"Back in the day—souping up old Chevelles and 'Cudas with the gang."

"The gang, hey?"

"You don't want to know about it, John."

"Do you have a reason why I shouldn't want to?"

"Certain places and times are not easily revisited, especially when shame is tied to them."

"If you think the timing isn't right, I can wait. But you will have to tell me sooner than later."

"Since the timing is never right for that kind of thing, I might as well get it over with. Hopefully the past doesn't define us, and as we've already explored, it can always be rewritten. I wasn't born in the best of setups, John. My environment in Mexico was toxic to say the least—not just the garbage, but the mindset, the criminal elements. When I said I never knew my father, it was a partial lie—I knew him alright. His absence was the result of my mother and me running away from his violence. Unfortunately, she didn't know any better than to associate with men just as bad as him, so when we finally got to San Francisco, it was through the same channels my father operated: drugs, coercion, blackmail, you name it, except that he wanted nothing to do with her at that point—he let her go for the whore she was in his mind. In a sense, she was lucky he saw her that way, otherwise he would have simply killed her in cold blood. When I became old enough to have sex and realized that rape was inevitable, I took charge. I read the boys before their hormones reached their perverted little brains. They were all rotten, even the good kids turned to shit after a certain age. So, I sexually provoked, enticed—I was good-looking enough for that—I could summon false confidence, but real enough for them to mistake it for the genuine item. I forced myself onto them with calculated fierceness, even though I was scared shitless on my first attempts. But they were too stupid to notice. I was never mistaken on the reality that it was still rape, I simply anticipated it and took the upper hand. Call it pride if you wish. Oddly, I gained their respect because of it, and they looked up to me in ways the other gals couldn't possibly dream of. I wished I could have helped the girls, but I was too busy trying to survive. In a world of reversed psychology, I became one of the guys on grounds of sheer toughness, all the while the victim of a lie, with primal fear as its base. I became one of the leaders, partook in criminal acts such as stealing cars, casing and robbing houses, blackmailing people into surrendering money, threatening to kill their children if they didn't comply. But when I reached seventeen, after getting pregnant and aborting the fetus, I had the epiphany that if I continued on that course, I was soon going to die. By then, I had already been drumming in hardcore bands, and so when the opportunity presented itself, me and one of the girls in the group who was my lover at the time, bailed out for Britain—you already know about that part. I didn't want to return—I knew I was going to be in trouble the minute I did. But then, I got news the gang got involved in an intrication with the police, resulting in the killing of four of the leaders and the arrest of most of the other members. When I made it back to the city, the coast was clear for a new life. By then, I had made the choice to never get involved with another man—but here you are! That's the short version, John."

"What about education?" he asked, bedazzled.

"Oh, I went to school and studied alright. My life was a lot more spread out than I'm making it sound. I'll tell you more as we go. For now, you sit on it and decide whether you still want to live with me or not."

"It changes nothing."

"Then, that past is already being rewritten."

"I wish I could say I had a history like yours, but my only shame is to have been reared properly."

"There's something to be said about the depraved side of conformity, but I'm fairly sure its evils are quite well behaved. Of course, who knows what kind of naughtiness exists behind the polished wainscot of proper upbringings. You would tell me, John, if you knew of it, wouldn't you?" she humored in an overdone English accent.

"Well, there was the occasional hazing, I suppose. And then, the time Mary Darmouth exposed her loosened knickers to a pimply freshman, partially revealing her labia, with the intent of making him involuntarily ejaculate in his trousers. Interestingly enough, they ended up marrying each other. But as far as me getting in trouble, I am only guilty of moral rectitude."

"Bleak but pastoral—I guess the immoral side of rectitude is in its intolerance towards anything that challenges its raison d'être, which sums up to legally robbing the poor and invading foreign countries for sport," she ventured.

"Ouch, but I wasn't speaking of the beast. That being said, there is a form of perversity to everything, if you want to take the concept to its extremes. Moral rectitude is indeed fully capable of engaging in sinister pursuits."

"What a poetic way of describing aristocratic criminality: the sinister—but noble—pursuit of riches!"

"I see we bypassed business for social science."

"More fun by far, John!"

"Speaking of fun, at some point I would very much like to explore the shame element of your story— seriously though."

"It's a big one to tackle, John, but I'm willing as long as you confess to the downside of having been raised by the book—that can't just exist in a vacuum. I bet the minute we let the air out of that jar, something's bound to crawl out."

"Lovely thought, dearest Patricia, I can't wait to see what that might be. But what do you say we check the oil dipstick of that car of yours?"

"Agreed—car, here we come!"

9 – THE NINTH DAY

The previous evening was spent going around the house and planning the future layout of the apartment Patricia and John would be sharing a couple of months down the road. It went without saying that there were immutable laws to the contract that couldn't be breached, such as the sanctities of both the upstairs art studio and the basement rehearsal and recording space. But there were two other rooms on the second story that offered the possibility of a more secluded office area for John's writing and studies, though at the cost of guest accommodation. There were many logistics that had their proper place in time; thus, they downscaled the planning to the more realistic essentials of finding room for John's belongings upon his arrival, as well as the basics of splitting expenses. They opted to go to bed on the earlier side, content to streamline the evening to watching Citizen Kane on DVD, while snacking on light fares and drinking herbal tea. They set up the alarm for 6:00 a.m.

The morning announced the arrival of a spectacular day with birdsongs in the lemon tree and the dance of sunrays around the bedroom. They took a shower together, made coffee, and served pancakes topped with fresh fruit and maple yogurt, and then prepared sandwiches to be added to the cooler. They were out of the house by nine, safely past heavy commuter traffic. There was nothing more magical than coming down Divisadero Street, overlooking a resplendent bay with Tiburon in the background, knowing that within minutes, one would be riding across the Golden Gate Bridge, on their way to beautiful Marin and Sonoma counties.

They had planned on making it to Drake's Beach by noon, allowing for ample time to leisure along the way and enjoy their last big day together, since, Thursday, John would essentially be preparing for his return trip to Britain scheduled for early Friday (Patricia had already promised to drive him to the airport.) John was particularly tuned in as they crossed the bay, since it was where he became aware of being in the dream in the company of another Patricia, in the body of a different John, but as he had somewhat anticipated, nothing came of it—no déja vu, no omnipresence of overlapping existences. They were in the now of their official reality, with absolutely nothing to sway them off course. He felt relieved.

"By the look of it, there is no present connection with our doubles," Patricia observed.

"It makes sense, since we would have to have caught them being aware of us having been aware of them, when obviously they weren't. Two separate realities, for which we were blessed to have been given the means to—short of a better word—compare, in order to define ourselves and our relationship."

"A bit early for mind twisters, but I think I know what you're saying. I'm glad we can move on knowing there's nothing to look for, and enjoy the day. That being said, it's gonna be difficult to not be anxious when we get to the stretch between Stinson Beach and Point Reyes Station, and later, the parking lot at Drake's," she confessed.

"Understandingly so, Patricia, I was somewhat uneasy crossing the bridge, but I don't imagine anything will happen in the other places. I'm fairly confident all pertinent information has already been handed to us."

"I'm inclined to agree, John."

"Just the odd question, Patricia—would you have volunteered the use of your car if we hadn't been quite as close, I mean, just a little less close, like the way our doubles appeared to have been?"

"The way you think is interesting—I bet you'd make a good investigator. I wonder if I would have mentioned the car if it hadn't fallen within the specificity of trust and commitment... It's a fine line, John—I'm not sure I have a clear answer for it, but my guess is that I would have done the same as the first time, that is, letting you rent a car, or sharing the cost of one."

"I was wondering, because I was always under the impression it was a rental. I remember vividly making that point in the dream—different cars, different realities. But since I didn't know you owned one at the time, I guess it's irrelevant, unless we know what model those two were driving, which brings us to this particular Nissan Altima. Since I was the pilot in the process of making sure the dream was real by trying to assess its substance in squeezing the steering wheel and tapping the console, I don't recall it was the same vehicle," John said, semi-convinced.

"And that brings us to what exactly, John, since we have already established it wasn't us?"

"I guess we're dealing with nuances—I would like to know how close the reality of the dream is to this very moment. Is it the one directly next to us, or are there others in between?"

"If you seek a quick answer, John, it's the one next to us, because I don't see the point of straddling a bunch of probabilities to find one amid the clutter, too far off for relevance. Existence is complex, but not as tricky as your mind is, dear one," she said, amused.

"Point well taken, but I'm satisfied with your answer—I just needed confirmation. It's particularly significant in my view to know where those two are positioned, because I'm now more inclined to pay attention to minute details."

"I'm with you, but I'm not sure why we're going there since you already said you believed all pertinent information had already been handed to us."

"It's just that since I mentioned it, a little voice in the back of my head has been telling me that I should keep an eye for signs that could trigger some of the info that we may have overlooked," John revealed.

"Interesting—I suppose I should do the same then."

"It's up to you, but we don't have to worry until we get to that stretch of Highway One."

"Then, let's change subjects—I'm ready to enjoy the ride. D'you want a blue chip with guacamole?" Patricia asked as she reached for the cooler in the back seat.

Somehow the idea of a blue chip with avocado sent John's mind reeling into a world of absurd comedy. He imagined John Cleese appearing in a waiter's outfit, one raised eyebrow, asking, "Who's getting the blue chip with guacamole?" Patricia looked at him, perplexed.

"Get away from that joke before it comes to bite you, John—is it a yes, or a no?"

"How did you guess?"

"A week knowing you is worth a lifetime!"

"That's what happens when you befriend a single-cell organism—nothing much there to start with—but yes please, I'm a taker for the blue corn chip and guac!"

"Keep your hands on the steering wheel, I will feed it to you," she ordered, as she scooped the dip.

She waited for the road to straighten.

"Open wide and don't inhale it!"

There were two more feedings before John begged for restrain until lunch break. Patricia concurred. They later pulled over, just ahead of Muir Beach, for the customary roadside leg-stretcher and discreet visit behind the bush, and then continued on along the coast towards Stinson Beach.

— o —

The coastal town came and went. Patricia had asked to stop before heading for Point Reyes Station, deeming it necessary to regroup her thoughts and memory of the dream if she were to focus on elements that might have been overlooked. Though, without knowing what they were, she felt hesitant to invest faith into finding anything. John, on the other hand, was more inclined to believe an item of logic would poke through.

They didn't recognize the place of the dream as much as they felt they had come to it.

"I think this is it," Patricia said, "do we stop, or keep going?"

"I say we go and get it over with," John replied.

He had barely finished his sentence when he noticed a car in the rearview mirror approaching rapidly. It only took seconds before the black Dodge Challenger SRT incongruously raced by them, forcing an incoming vehicle to slow down.

"What was that?" John asked, incredulous.

"That was me back in the gang!"

"No wonder you thought you were going to die. But seriously, is there any rationale to acting in such a way so early in the day?"

"Time becomes irrelevant after you cross the line. These guys could still be on last night's binge, or already well advanced into their next party—miscreants on their way to burn—I'm familiar with the psychological profile."

"I don't remember that in the dream."

"Neither do I, but we could still be ahead of time—I don't believe we're quite there yet."

"I thought you said we were..."

"Anticipation can play tricks on the mind."

But then, it all came into focus—the exact moment the two recognized their simultaneous presence in the dream.

"Talk about déja vu, John, this is massive. I feel so close to that experience, it's insane. They must be right next to us, barely a space unit away from us."

"A space unit—I love it! Indeed, we could easily be in the process of connecting with our dream selves, presently in that reality."

"What an odd concept, but I see what you mean."

"Now is the time to pay particular attention to hidden items," John suggested.

"All sensors and antennas out!"

John chuckled.

But then something occurred—the two realities, almost imperceptively, merged into one, just long enough for John to hear Patricia say, "I still can't believe that crazy driver," and for Patricia to see John nod in acknowledgement. And then, it was gone.

"OK, sweetie, I don't remember hearing you state that in the dream, but somehow, it resonates."

"It's because we were observers, she must have said it nonetheless. I'm convinced that very last moment was common to both places—we fucking merged, or crossed!" she exclaimed, astonished at the realization.

"It appears so—being prepared for it probably helped with the revelation. But I believe we are now past the dream stretch."

"I have the distinct feeling our doubles thought nothing of it—they must have been merely commenting on what had just happened," she said.

"Which makes it all the more significant at our end, if you get my logic."

"At least, worth keeping an eye for, just in case that speeder comes back the other way," she warned.

"Another thing that arose for me—I am now of the belief our copies are driving your car as well."

"I thought you had ascertained it was a rental."

"I am reevaluating that assertion."

"What gave?"

"The dream came into clearer focus when our two realities crossed—it was the same car."

"How important is that?" she asked.

"It is all in knowing how closely we parallel each other. I suspect our friends are more tightly connected than we first thought. For that reason, I trust we have to keep our worlds from getting too close."

"Are you inferring that merging would be bad?"

"I am saying there is a reason why we now exist in separate realities—the outcomes are likely to be radically different. I strongly believe we have no business going where those two are bound to."

"How do you propose we do that, John?"

"By staying true to the course and trusting that we exist within the best possible scenario, love."

"I second that, John, thank you. It appears your department of intuition has been gaining in confidence rather rapidly—congratulations!"

"It's difficult for me to keep the scientific mind out of it, but I try my best, Patricia."

"At any rate, I think we can now resume with the trip as planned. Remember, it's supposed to be a special celebration."

"I concur—the day is still young!"

— o —

The quality of the late morning drive along coastal Highway One, or Shoreline Highway as it was also known, was enhanced by clear skies and crisp air. They drove with the windows down, taking in the smell of star thistle and eucalyptus, intermixed with the salts of Bolinas Lagoon. Following the seventeen mile inland stretch that tied the lagoon to Tomales Bay, along the San Andreas Fault Line separating the Point Reyes Peninsula from the continental mass, they turned left on Sir Francis Drake and made for the town of Inverness. They parked the Altima by the Shaker furniture shop, a small rustic house opened in 1975 by Barbara Williams and her husband, Thomas, and the first of its kind since the closure of the New Lebanon chair factory in the early forties. Patricia was particularly fond of the sober design of Shaker furniture. It was stark, bordering on severe, but carried a mystique that, according to her, translated as a form of spiritual craft, defined by removing all that was deemed unessential. Her house was adorned with specimens bought from the very shop, more for display than use, for she claimed that their presence appeased her mind in moments of stress. John was delighted by the new information. Even though the Shakers originated from England, he only knew little of them. Although, their progressive thinking in regard to the equality of the sexes, and the leading role of women in the sect had come to his attention during his studies, he had no idea they built furniture. Of course, the Williamses, by being married, did not abide to the Shakers' vow of celibacy, but that was inconsequential in the context of the revival of one of the group's legacies, as it neared its inevitable demise.

Patricia and John agreed lunchtime was approaching. They opted to set camp at the next picnic area, a place oddly named Chicken Ranch Beach, on the Tomales Bay. In the distance, a group of elks were grazing, inconspicuous to the fact that the increase in human presence in the area on a weekday was caused by an observance in honor of secretaries, which some blissfully confused for a public holiday, while others despised it as demeaning to those it purposed to show its appreciation. That being said, the elks didn't care.

The guacamole was promptly consumed and followed by the smoked tofu, shredded carrots, and spring greens sandwiches. Before long, they were leisurely on their way to their destination, occasionally pulling over to make room for the faster drivers. Eventually, Patricia found herself at the place of the last of the conscious dreams, in the parking lot above Drake's Beach.

Something uncanny immediately jumped at the two—the Challenger that has passed them earlier, and the

Dodge Ram pickup truck that had smoked them on Sloat Boulevard a few days prior, and whose license plate number Patricia had memorized, were parked side by side.

"Don't tell me those guys are going to make a misery out of the day," she complained.

"We won't let them. I'm fairly sure they aren't as far in as we're going to be, and, perhaps, they went the other direction."

"You're right—I'm not going to let my mind play into their bullshit. There's a lesson in there for me," she conceded.

John was correct. When they reached the bottom of the trail, a group of six men, a short distance to the right, had cleared an area the size of a small plaza, at the center of which they were seen gesticulating jerkily, and heard shouting belligerent remarks in drunken and otherwise impaired tones.

"These idiots are not only drinking hard shit, they're also on meth," Patricia uttered.

"In my field of neurology, some of the colleagues refer to it as the *explosive mix*—another way of saying the *neuron blaster*."

"About right—good thing we're going left!"

"Isn't now and here the time and place of your last conscious dream?"

"Yes, and it was also when you first mentioned about your meeting with your colleagues, and the low prospects of finding a job in your field in the Bay Area."

"Well, if that's all there is, it settles it then—time to find our spot in the sun!"

The beach, along which it was believed Sir Francis Drake had moored the *Golden Hind* for repairs, was a long stretch of sand walled by mudstone cliffs, whose full length was only traveled by dedicated walkers, who, as it turned out, were in short supply on that particular afternoon. It didn't take very long for Patricia and John to establish safe distance and eventually find the perfect area to settle, out of sight. They had brought water—John didn't have to ask. Patricia understood, then, that the two realities were, at last, significantly shifting from each other. There was no longer a need to look for messages, or heed to the unexpected. She was relieved, sensing John was too. They stripped naked, took a quick dip in the frigid waters of Drake's Bay, spread towels on the sand, and lay on their backs to dry off under the rays. John was first to offer the customary oil rub, which was followed by coaxing reciprocation, and then love-making. An errant couple who had come to the beach, likely for similar reasons as the two, walked by, pretending they hadn't noticed, conspiratorially approving of the act with subtle chuckles. Patricia and John never saw them. After passions cooled off, aided by another dip in the sobering coldness of the brine, John pulled a tiny box out of his daypack, opened it, and while he fell to one knee, asked Patricia in marriage.

"Before I answer to that, allow me to compliment you on your style—how princely of you in all of your naked glory! So, it's a yes, John, you may marry me!" she exclaimed with laughter.

He slipped the ring around her finger – she didn't mind the entire thing was made of plastic. He deemed her not to be the diamond type, so he proposed that they look together for something she would love.

"You shouldn't have splurged, hon, but you're right, I have tastes that veer off the norm," she humored.

"I could tell by the Sundance catalog in your bathroom."

"That's still kinda normative, but I like some of their stuff."

"Perhaps tomorrow we can look for something in town?"

"You know what, John; when back in Cambridge, pick one that will suit the Patricia of your heart—I'm sure she will love it. Until then, this ring will do just fine, if you don't mind me keeping it on display among the sacred items on my altar."

It was a simple engagement, manifest in its sincerity, yet playful and stripped of unreasonable expectations. They gave their best to trust and the faith that there was ample integrity and goodness in each of them to go the full length of their promise to spend a lifetime together. It was a deal straight from the heart.

— o —

When Patricia and John later came to the bottom of the trail, the party animals had left the premises. The observation was punctuated by an engine roar, the squealing of spinning tires, and a cloud of black soot rising from the parking lot above. The commotion settled with the distancing of a monotonal, subsonic, thumping pulse. When they arrived at the flat, next to where the offending vehicles had been parked, the asphalt was littered with broken glass bottles and other rubbish dripping with urine—the boys had marked their territory.

"I don't think these idiots will make it back to wherever they came from in one piece," Patricia said.

"With that level of attention-seeking, it's unlikely they won't come to a head with the park rangers or the highway patrol," John added.

"That would be the best case scenario for everyone, but I know too well that only a catastrophic situation will put an end to their spiral of misdeeds. The mission gangs lost many members to similar recklessness—I came close to being one of them."

"Would you have urinated outside your own vehicle in a public car park?" John asked, incredulous.

"Of course, with that kind of inebriation, I probably exposed myself with extreme indecency on more than one occasion. Fear and anger breed vulgarity, but that would have been the least of my evils, John— nothing to be proud of, really."

"I'm afraid to ask what the greater evils were."

"So, just don't ask, my sweet man—this girl is already having a hard time living with the memory. The idea of unloading some of it now might prove too toxic on such a sacred day. I will answer all your questions in due time—promised."

"Now you are making it impossible for me not to come back," he teased.

"That was part of the plan the minute I picked you up at the airport."

"A mere pawn in a nefarious ploy!" he cried.

— o —

By the time they drove through Inverness, Patricia and John had long forgotten about the parking lot incident. They agreed to return to Terrapin Crossroads for dinner, and perhaps hang out to catch one of the shows.

The one hiccup was to decide which of the many ways to take to get there. In the end, they chose, on John's recommendation, to return to Stinson Beach and take the Panoramic Highway to Mount Tamalpais, for a spectacular view of San Francisco and the bay. But when they came to one of the tight hairpins in the road, highway patrol cars and fire trucks, all lights flashing, were busy on the steep side, attending to a wreck down the slope, where a fire was seen raging and from which black smoke erupted in thick plumes. Traffic was quickly ushered along by efficient personnel intent on preventing rubber-necking. But not too far up the hill, a parking area provided a clear view of the accident, from which Patricia and John recognized, out of the three heavily mangled vehicles, the two from the Drake's Beach parking lot. The Dodge Challenger that had passed them in the morning was the one aflame. By the look of it, it was unlikely anyone had made it. As it turned out, the third car, which was coming from the opposite direction when the two racing vehicles came speeding around the corner on the wrong side, was clipped and spun around into a death dance, before plunging down the steep ravine with the other two. It was the end of the wild party for the boys— the last stop of their mean-spirited and utterly pointless life-daring rampage.

— o —

But there was another version to the story—one in which a fourth vehicle, a beige 2004 Nissan Altima, was also involved in the crash. The two passengers, an Englishman from Cambridge, and a woman from the Mission district of San Francisco were pronounced dead at the scene. They had just returned from Drake's Beach where they had sex, but John hadn't pulled a small box out of his daypack, and slipped a plastic ring around Patricia's finger to ask her in marriage. They had taken off earlier and were gone before the two suspect vehicles had even left the lot. When they came onto the fatal turn on Panoramic Highway, the racing car and truck arrived from behind, horns blaring. The first one passed them at high speed, but as it crashed into the incoming traffic, the second one, overreacting to avoid the wreck, lost control and sideswiped Patricia's car, forcing it violently off the road. All four vehicles came tumbling down the rocky slope, in a cacophony of crushed and torn metal. The Challenger caught on fire. There were no survivors.

Up a small distance, at the edge of the parking area from which the accident was visible, before Highway Patrol cars and fire engines would eventually arrive, John and Patricia stood—watching.

John: "Well, I suppose that's how it had to end for these two."

Patricia: "Quite so, I didn't expect it would be easy for them. She intuitively knew he wouldn't be able to return, and though she chose to believe, on the strength of their connection, that he would act on his word, she was ultimately aware something was amiss at the deeper trust levels."

John: "Even though he wanted to move in with her, she recognized how he had kept her at a safe distance from the reality of his tethers to his job at the University of Cambridge, irreversibly negating the space for full trust to come between them—a voluntary blindness on his part, as we know. But of course, there was the dream that came to the others' help."

Patricia: "Naturally, the dream was only possible because those two had already created the level of trust necessary to open the doors of perception. Their willingness to face their fears was testament of their respective dedication to seeing across the limiting line."

John: "In your opinion, what was the point at which the reality of the original pair split into two distinct courses?"

Patricia: "I don't think there was a clear break—they seemed to be going back and forth for a while, splitting, remerging, and splitting again... But from my angle, it happened before the dream, while on their walk under the moon when Patricia recognized her feelings for John, and prolonged the exposure of her aroused senses to him. That was when she broke loose from some of the limitations she had set for herself."

John: "Certainly, there were other factors, since they ended up being lovers in both realities."

Patricia: "It was a blurred line where both versions acted as one, but a clear, unspoken choice was made during the meeting on Monday, when our John, down there, wasn't as strong about the job rebuttal as his counterpart was. In that reality, they didn't take their lunch at the Sloat Boulevard café, where the other two witnessed the inconspicuously pivotal incident of the soot-emitting pickup truck—he never came to share his thoughts about that meeting until today at the beach. By the time they met later that Monday, the two courses had reached a permanent state of separation. The crossing of the two realities on Highway 1, after that car passed them this morning, was a momentary convergence for the purpose of handing information to the couple about to come upon their version of this accident."

Patricia: "So, you're saying the meeting was the decisive moment of the split?"

John: "In appearance, yes, but the dream happened before it; hence, separate courses were already in play. It's quite plausible that items preceding their joining at the airport were active, ready to set the tone for variations on the theme to occur."

Patricia: "But that was the result of them rewriting the past as they became closer—they were aware of *the shifts* and how they affected time in both direction."

John: "Yes, there is that—unequivocally—looking at it from the spacious present. But I believe we are here to review the linearity of the physical experience."

Patricia, laughing: "As we always do, but we aren't them—yet we are. Nonetheless, the point is well taken!"

John: "As we know, there are other scenarios, but this one here is closest to our favorite in which this version of us is doing extremely well—we have reason to be proud of those two, have we not?"

Patricia: "Proud is an understatement when we feel they are practically us. Their growth is quite spectacular and it promises to go exponentially from there—I think we did well, my dear friend."

"Thank you—I concur!"

Naturally, it wasn't really John and Patricia standing on that edge, or rather, they were different ones—more complete ones—the ones that were encompassment of all the Patricias and Johns of the many realities they inhabited. The one difference between the two main couples was that one went the extra length in trust and faith. They earned and owned their relationship, because they were willing to explore a difficult, but not so unrealistic unknown—that of removing all preconceived notions of disempowerment. Trust was the path to love, and love to more trust, and for that reason, time made room for a little engagement ritual on the beach, that was just long enough to push trouble out of the way. Of course, all the players had to act their parts—good guys and bad ones alike. So, nothing was really ever cast in stone, as most of the time, things were not as they appeared. But that was beyond the point, since John and Patricia were no longer standing at the edge of the slope, while police cars, fire engines, and ambulances were arriving amid great tumult.

— o —

"So, sweetie, off to Terrapin Crossroads?" Patricia asked, still somewhat shaken, as the Nissan pulled out of the parking area.

"On our way, my love, and who knows, we may even dine with Phil tonight!"

"I don't doubt it—everything's possible with you around, my dear man!"

10 – THE TENTH DAY

There was a dream, one in which Patricia was speaking with John, as they watched the spectacle of the accident from the vantage point of the small pullout, higher up on the winding road. But there was no car next to them, no Nissan Altima—instead it rested at the bottom of the ravine amid twisted metal, nearly unrecognizable.

"What do you make of this, John?"

"They chose to end it here. I am rejoiced the other two did well—time to move on!" he replied tonelessly.

It was all Patricia remembered when she woke up, her heart racing. She sat up in the bed. John stirred and switched the light on, lovingly worried.

"What's going on, sweetie—are you alright?"

"I think I know what happened to the other two!"

"What did?"

"They died in that crash—I saw our car with the other three at the bottom. You and I were exactly where we stood when we watched, except we weren't us—definitely not them either... Perhaps, in the end, we're all one, John... I'm so fucking confused!"

"Do you want me to fetch a glass of water?"

"No thanks, I need to use the bathroom anyway—I think I'm about to menstruate. I'm normally a full moon girl but I'm slightly behind this month—all that great love-making," she said, released from the disorienting effect of the dream.

"I thought there was no relation between period and moon cycles!" he uttered from the distance of the bed.

"Go tell the girls, cowboy, I'm sure they'll remind you where you belong!"

"From the medical end, it's considered a faulty science at best!"

"Whatever the medical end says, John! For your information, *mene* means moon, and *menses* means month, as in Greek and Latin. Remember Greek and Latin, John?!"

"But it's well documented that ovulation and period are not dependent on full and new moons..." John insisted, as Patricia returned from the bathroom.

"It's nothing but an uphill battle for you, my dear man—just let it go and I will pretend we never had this conversation."

"OK then, I'll take one in the name of further education," he willingly surrendered.

"Good, now, let's go back to sleep before the world awakens," she said, kissing John on the forehead.

— o —

After a copious breakfast set in the sun-soaked backyard, the topic of Patricia's dream came back to the table. They had briefly spoken about it upon getting up, but she had felt uneasy exploring its meaning while she was still in the process of adjusting to reality.

"So, it's reasonable to conclude our doubles died at the hands of the maniacs after returning from the beach, is that right?" John unwrapped.

"Yeah, those fools were kind of a marker along the way, but little did we know how close they came to taking us as well. I guess, the main difference was that we stayed at the beach longer, which probably means our doubles didn't have an engagement ceremony."

"Good point—of course, that would mean all the elements played on similar timetables due to the close proximity of the two realities."

"In the end, it's a victory for trust and the thirst for adventure. Thinking of it, we had many an excuse to not make the extra step, but we chose to listen to our inner longings instead of walking away. Remember, there were a couple of times when we seriously thought of not pursuing our connection. I believe the other two existed in a reality in between," Patricia voiced.

"Just to prove the best-case scenario is always along the path of least resistance. It all boils down to the willingness to admit that most personal hurdles are constructs of the mind, the tallest of which being to doubt the self's ability to remove them."

"Right on—as I've preached since leaving my gang days behind—there is no room for bullshit in a sane world!"

"A sound conclusion! More coffee, my love?"

I I - BEYOND

Patricia drove John to the airport early that Friday. They parted after a long embrace, knowing it was only a matter of time before their lives would rejoin for a lasting walk to the finish. Although their energies were already intertwined, but perhaps because it was true that absence made the heart grow fonder, Patricia knew she wouldn't find relief until at last, John dropped his bags onto the floor of the apartment. She cried as he walked through the gate.

John quit his university job. He was turned down for early retirement, but he didn't care—the money would come through in due time. He sold the Cambridge house rather than rent it and have to deal with picky tenants and the odd plumbing repair from across the globe. His publisher was supportive of his choice to dedicate more time to writing, and actually welcomed the idea of straying from his previous work in favor of more radical subjects and territories.

As anticipated, the resistance to see him depart carried the sweet and sour of concealed resentments, especially in his department, where the desertion rankled in the reverberating halls like a wound to its ancient pride. The old pub friends sagged to the news, as if afflicted by a severance of contract, but he imagined that, one day, they would forego their discomfort, to elevate the name of John Leeds to the mystique of those who dared wander into the foreboding unknowns. Most likely, they would forget about him altogether.

Contrarily to the persistent rumors of gruesome delays in dealing with the U.S. immigration services, the processing of John's fiancé visa was, at worst, a mild procedural tedium. As long as he and Patricia were married within the allotted period, the rest would lie on following through with appointments and paperwork.

Amusingly, he received an email from UCSF's Max Dawson with the offer of a post, just to prove, once again, that the mind set the path of least resistance by remaining the observer. He smiled at the comforting irony. Perhaps, he would give it a chance after all.

— o —

Immediately after leaving John at the airport, Patricia experienced an existential void. She realized that her life, in spite of its semblance of stability, had been a long battle followed by years of healing. Though, her strength had been in taking charge of her private struggles, self-empowerment wasn't at the exclusion of facing adversity, or in denying the inner demons their place in the sun. However, she felt she had come to a close. Perhaps all it took was an ally to help open all the doors and let go of what was pushing against them. It had been ten days that felt like years, as if in that short time, her entire life had unraveled and reorganized itself.

But beyond the sense of visceral loss, her thoughts had become clearer, her purpose more defined. She would dedicate her energy to the creative process, drum, paint, write—live her life on a grand canvas, the one of her heart, and deeper into the layers, the one of a more mysterious reality from which all she knew and accomplished sprang. She cried nearly all the way to the garage, where she parked the Nissan with the promise to revisit the places she and John had seen together.

They hadn't quite dined with Phil Lesh the evening of the accident, but he had stopped by their table to thank them for their patronage, lingering some after noticing John was British and hearing that Patricia was in an all-female drum group. He took her card with the promise of putting her in touch with friends in the business. She had heard it all before, but when the call came, she realized it was for real. A meeting was followed by an audition and a series of recording sessions with various incarnations composed of the many friends that perpetuated the tradition of the San Francisco sound. The work helped alleviate her yearning for John's presence, ground her into the now by allowing her to surrender to the joy of creating new life through beats. She also noticed that the sale of her books had picked up on Amazon, as more reviews popped up. It was a modest income, but an income all the same that delighted her by its sudden occurrence. On top of it, she had sold two paintings and was told there was mounting interest in her work. She didn't have to rationalize on the reasons why all of it was converging into a positive whole—she understood it intuitively. There was no room for the mind to cast its shadow over the moving tapestry it was only meant to watch and appreciate. So, she relaxed into her natural position of being one with the source of her existence, and prepared herself to be mesmerized.

— o —

At long last, John dropped his bags on the floor of the apartment. It took just over two months for him to put order to his things. There had been no procrastinating, no excuses, no remorse. He recognized he had made the most valuable choice of his entire life, the one of validating his deeper aspirations by accepting the notion that roadblocks were only temporary. Even outside resistance had been his all along—a reflection of his inner conflicts and angsts. He was free, while at the same time, coming home. Patricia almost refrained from touching him, fearing to be overcome by emotions and breaking the sanctity of a private moment that belonged to a slightly later time. But, as it turned out, the present wanted nothing of it, and so they kissed passionately in the entryway, the door slightly ajar onto the busy street, and then made straight for the bedroom. There would be plenty of time to unpack.

END

OTHER WORKS BY THE AUTHOR

The Disappearance of Olaf Swyndle
(Book 1 of An Improbable Emergence)

The Hektor Dilemma
(Book 2 of An Improbable Emergence)

Ma-l's Grand Gathering
(Book 3 of An Improbable Emergence)

Convergence of the Realms
(Book 4 of An Improbable Emergence)

Escape from Inconsequence

Story of a Tale-Maker

Nine Amber Pieces

A Life Given, a Life Taken

Hello! My Name is Tunes

A Cycle of Falls

francisvoignier.com
Dolosse & Writs, Eureka, California

.